SITA IN EXILE

SITA

IN

EXILE

Rashi Rohatgi

MIAMI UNIVERSITY PRESS

Copyright © 2023 by Rashi Rohatgi

Library of Congress Cataloging-in-Publication Data

Names: Rohatgi, Rashi, author.

Title: Sita in exile / Rashi Rohatgi.

Description: Oxford, Ohio : Miami University Press, [2023]

Identifiers: LCCN 2022046835 | ISBN 9781881163725 (paperback)

Subjects: LCGFT: Novellas.

Classification: LCC PS3618.O4855 S58 2023 | DDC 813/.6—dc23/eng/20221107

LC record available at https://lccn.loc.gov/2022046835

Designed by Crisis

Printed in Michigan on acid-free, recycled paper

Miami University Press

356 Bachelor Hall

Oxford, Ohio 45056

TO ALL MY LV AUNTIES,
AND TO THEIR DAUGHTERS

PART ONE

1

The sun was horrific. It spread itself over the fjord like an overturned pot of buttermilk, ready to be lapped up by a tiny, mischievous god. Sita wondered if Bhoomija was watching the sun set over the Midwest. Everyone between them was asleep.

Except Mona, who was calling out to her from higher up the mountain, where there was supposedly a lake. Sita turned her back to the sun and pushed herself forward, trying to smile. It wasn't entirely Mona's fault she couldn't pronounce her name; no one here could say "th." Morten must have heard Pierre say it at least once a day—Sita didn't have a good read on how often her husband complained about her at work—and hadn't even tried, had told her, first thing when they'd met last night, that he was going to call her Stella. "I give everyone nicknames," he'd explained, handing her a hot dog she cradled limp in her hands for the rest of the night, "like this one: I call her Luna, for lunatic."

"So you can see, we're already a pair," said Mona.

When was the last time anyone had extended their hand to her? She took hold of the giant palm, proportional to the giant woman who might have warned her to bring sunglasses. Pulled in, she saw the promised lake, and wanted to cry but recognized she must stop herself. Pierre had closed the door softly when he'd come home last night, from work and then afterwork drinks with Morten and others he'd only told her about. "Please," he said, pulling the needles from her hands and setting them on the counter. "If you wanted a proper quarantine, you've done it. Let's go out."

Hindus only mourned for thirteen days, she conceded, but she didn't explain. Instead she'd set down her half-formed hat still on its needles and pulled on a bra and the red scarf she'd been wearing the night they'd met and had worn since, lest he find her skin sallow without it, and followed him out into the bright spring evening.

She'd felt her shoulders shaking throughout the grilling, and she found herself shaking now. There was a bench on the far side of the lake, but Mona pulled her to a flat stone and waved her hand to tell her she must sit upon it. Sita unfurled her scarf and swung it round herself again and bent her knees and hugged them. Their backs were turned to the fjord, and Sita counted the days in her head until the full moon. Yes, it was. Mona laid her butter-yellow hijab on the vinalon of her canary-yellow bag and stared at the same mountains she must have looked at every Holi of her life. "So, Sita," she said, "tell me the story of your scarf."

She tried to organize, in thought and then word, what she might say about the paisley pattern, the apologies she might make for the stitches she'd dropped at eighteen, but all she could feel was the body it protected, her soul covered by skin she hardly recognized, protected by flesh that felt suffocating, inoperative valves stuck to her chest. She shook her head, and then bent her chin to the peak that remained ahead. Snow lingered as though cloud.

"Next time," said Mona, though Sita would push off Mona's invitations all summer. Issued as they were via Pierre via Morten, this was easy. It was answering the question that was difficult.

2

If she'd had her way he wouldn't have learned to speak at all. His eyes seemed fully grown already, irises big and black as olives, and as they orbited one another in the kitchen, she understood that he had begun to know her: he'd seen the way her knuckles trembled just before she pushed on the power to the food processor, the way she'd eat the onions cut every afternoon after puja layer by layer, a tearful prasad. She'd known that firangis kept animals in their homes—had even known a more assimilated auntie and uncle who'd kept a dog, its white hair coating the living room—and so knew any arguments would ultimately be overruled. And of course if they set the mongoose free it would die, immediately and desperately, in the early autumn frost. So Nenn was here, and every evening, while she retired to the computer to exchange banal messages with her distracted friends during their lunch breaks, she would listen to Pierre read to their new

housemate from the local papers. Slowly. Repeating preposi-
tional phrases, to remember them.

She didn't speak to Nenn, but he quickly adapted himself to
the daily routine. There were four shops, all of them full of over-
priced and pointless items: banker's lamps, huge flanks of mut-
ton. He sat in pen pocket of her t-shirt, body bundled underneath
the thick-knit sweater, head almost wrapped up in the end of her
red paisley scarf. Neither of them said anything inside of the
stores. Then: the harbor. They'd learned not to come around lunch
hour, when the shrimp man came to offload his catch and when
peons from the offices nearby made their way from green-glassed
block to wooden restaurant and back again. Otherwise it was
quiet, most of the boats out, the lighthouse blinking seemingly
haphazardly, though Sita didn't see how this could be the case.
If the heat from his tiny mass didn't radiate far enough throughout her being to warm her fingertips, they'd stop at the mosque
and leave a coin in the dropbox next to the carafe, and pour the
coffee into the empty travel mug emblazoned with the logo of her
erstwhile employer. She'd hold it between her mittens until they
reached the top of hill at the outskirts of the village, a way station of green before houses gave way to proper stone mountains,
before roads gave way to proper trails. They'd watch the islands
float in the distance as she drank, or didn't drink, east first, then
south, then north, and then Nenn would nod and they'd descend,

straight back home, shaking off their garments and lighting the stove to heat water to thaw them. If there was a package for Pierre, they would leave the contents on his nightstand and she would give the box to Nenn as though he were a child in addition to being child-sized, or really infant-sized. He would examine it with respect and sometimes, when she came out of the bedroom in the morning, she'd find him sleeping in it.

On the fifth week after his arrival, after the puja tears, he told her he was going for a walk, and would she please leave the door slightly ajar, as he couldn't reach the door handle. "Ji," she said, and before thinking better of it or further about it, watched him slink out, without even socks or a hat against the chill.

For a few days after that she was wary of him, unable to determine whose responsibility it was to speak next. She couldn't make herself doubt what she'd seen and heard: otherwise, her whole life might collapse. But until she decided whether or not she wanted this conversation to continue she refrained from praying or singing out loud. There was no other way Nenn could have learned Hindi, unless he spent his nights reading through her neglected, though dearly delivered, library. She didn't think he had the thumbs to do so, but then, she had assumed his coat was scant protection, and he'd gallivanted for almost an hour uncovered. Instead of praying, singing bhajans, or crying, she spent that time knitting for him. Pierre asked her to knit a hat for him, too, but she rolled her eyes. He wore a size easily available, and owned several machine-knit hats, his favorite of which was emblazoned with the same logo as her coffee mug. He'd liked to joke that it was a gender-swapped letter jacket, but found himself unable to adapt that material to local conditions. On the fourth day she left the finished set of knitwear—orange and green, Marius-patterned—next to Nenn's current sleeping box, and the next day she helped him into it and watched him go for another walk.

Finally she was charmed by the realization that he was waiting for her to decide whether or not she wanted to talk, that he would not impinge upon her mental space until she signaled acquiescence or even eagerness. The day was Chhoti Diwali, anyway, so it would have been strange not to perform her puja. When she began to sing, asking Bhagwan to give her mental strength, she paused to glance to her left. Nenn was singing with her. Now that she had the wherewithal to listen, she found that his voice was soft and clear, not at all chipmunk-like, as she had expected, but very much as solemn as she had imagined.

They exchanged a few sentences, maximum, after that, never during their outings, and usually not until that fallow space between her tears and ten minutes before Pierre's anticipated return, when she began dinner preparation. She couldn't, she explained, ask Nenn questions the way he liked to ask her; she knew that if she began to discern the inner life of a mongoose she'd have gone mad, and she preferred to avoid that. So Nenn asked questions, and would wait for her answer, and sometimes in response to her reply his eyes would darken, or gleam, or widen, but he always trusted that the response she gave was the full response she was going to provide. Gradually, she began to breathe more easily, knowing that, cold as she was, Pierre had given her a family.

*

As the moon waxed anew, Sita told Nenn about trick-or-treating. At first, she described to him the gloomy walks through her natal neighborhood canvassing for UNICEF, freezing in her determination not to cover her princess costume. As she lifted the lengha up for him from its tissue-papered box, a spangled satin set she'd worn to every formal event before and after puberty, she'd explained that despite her embarrassment in front of the snakes dressed up as cats—no, metaphorically, she promised, as the tips of his eyes narrowed—she'd loved the way they gaped at the bare midriff she was allowed to display. And later, when she'd met Pierre at a Halloween party her first year in the city, though she didn't say so, she'd loved the way he'd gaped, too.

By the empty afternoon at the month's end, the village had become dark and its surface icy, and Sita, having no purchase on it, was constrained to only those paths others had found worth walking on and salted. Nenn strained against her pocket, paw on his brow against the reflected sun, determined to enact a posada of disguised mirth. They'd spent the sunlit hours scouring the shops for toy bears wearing aviators; he needed the small glasses for his Amelia Earhart costume. As she'd known, there weren't any—there hadn't been any yesterday, and no ships had come in since—but Sita had felt Nenn's heart pulsing and felt there was no option.

She felt whipped frozen and appropriately dressed all at once, her navel only protected, as Nenn was, by the lengha's orni instead of her customary red scarf. It wasn't a concession to the mongoose's fervor but rather in response to the quiver she felt in her over-exposed stomach. Though he hadn't spoken yet to Pierre, she could sense it was only a matter of time, of a change in season, and the season was changing clearly now. She'd begun buying vegetables frozen to avoid the window above the sink, out of which bolts of emerald, bright and thin as chiffon, flung through the sky disconsolate and angry at being left behind with nothing but the darkness for company. Nenn would leave her then, sometimes not bothering to wrap up in the scarves she'd prepared for him by now in every color, every pattern she knew how to make, and would come back when Pierre did, when the peas were again plump and the rice fattened, the freshly chopped onions coated in chonk. Sita did not know how to stop their alliance, and had an inchoate idea that to try to would be not only churlish but sinful.

They argued that night, dressing, not for a night of revelry but at least a shared nod to nostalgia at the gossipy pub: Pierre had bought a yellow sweatshirt and yellow hat and she had to explain that Nenn had his own ideas, that he didn't want to pretend to be a small monkey unless he could be a small monkey wearing a leather jacket sewn together out of her once-fanciest gloves, as well as her orni knotted into an ascot. By the time she explained that she couldn't be the monkey, either, obviously, Pierre's pacing had made it impossible for her to do anything but stand as still as possible and close her eyes.

"Sita can wear the yellow, and you can be the monkey."

If Pierre was going to throw Nenn against the wall, she was going to keep her eyes closed. But there was silence—finally—and then Pierre's warm, sleepy laugh. When she looked, Pierre was tossing Nenn up in the air like a volleyball. "Okay, champ, now that is a good idea." He placed him tenderly on the kitchen island next to her shivling and peeled the sweatshirt off. He was wearing a brown Henley underneath that Sita had to admit would do well for a monkey, but when he saw her face he winked and peeled that off, too. "Give us a minute or twenty."

She couldn't concentrate, though she tried, on the dance of his fingers against her thighs. "Mon loup," she murmured, but instead of responding he increased his pace, his pressure, and she gave up, but when it was over and she waited for him to get out of the shower, she found the question still clutching at her heart: had he known Nenn's secret all along, and let her cling to it for warmth? Or did he simply not care what she thought?

Nenn was quiet as they slipped down to the pub, a small respite. They stood at a corner table nodding constantly to Pierre's coworkers, who'd inevitably wave him over rather than approach what, she had to assume, they thought was a rodent rather than a herpestine. To compensate, she let Nenn take sips of her plum porter. By the end of the evening he was swaying on the table, and she giggled. "You look like the lights," she told him.

"You look like a princess," he said, and she hadn't the heart not to weep.

"My lovelies," said Pierre, placing himself between them, one hand gripping two full mugs, leaving the other free to stroke Nenn's tail. "Have we gotten to the sad part, then?"

On the walk home, the wind whistled through the gaps between their clasped fingers; the moon, she told Nenn—riding, as he'd come, atop Pierre's shoulder—was made of cheese, or so she'd been told in her turn. Whatever spirits traveled between the veils tonight were mellow, and the streetlights led them to where they belonged. As she spoke to him, her tears turned to hail on her face, and fell, crushing the leaves beneath her feet. When she was finished Pierre taught Nenn the song he sang Sita at the end of every costume party they'd co-opted in celebration of their love, a song about dismembering birds that reminded him he was hungry. She wanted to pluck Nenn from his shoulder to stop him joining Pierre for a kebab, but instead she let herself into the house and decided it was time to buy curtains.

The next morning, snow blanketed the iced cobbles, and Sita made her way up the hill with her diminutive companion, though Nenn never spoke to her again. By Christmas, by which Sita was sure she was pregnant, she wasn't sure if he ever had.

3

Pierre and Nenn were undaunted by the rain. They had hats, it was true—she'd made red, white, and blue beanies for the three of them, seed stitched—but mostly, Pierre loved a chance to dress up. He took her lengha out of the closet and brought it into the kitchen and interrupted her offering; as he tapped her elbow, her wrist shook and the milk escaped the ablution channel and bled onto the counter. "One more chance to wear this," he whispered in her ear, as Nenn lapped up the excess.

"It gets heavy when it's wet," she protested, aloud—they were alone in the house—and left the milk on the counter, just for a second, just until it was clear that Pierre wouldn't replace it for her. She hated opening the fridge these days: she was constantly cold, constantly trembling as though the fetus inside was churning her, shaping her as it wished instead of the other way around. Inside the fridge, next to the milk, sat three bottles of red. She'd thought of her best friend Bhoomija, thought how pleased she'd be to find Sita free of red, white, and blue as shorthand for American imperialism. It would require a bit of a finessing, to be sure, an intro speech about how this would be an opportunity for her to prove she could be a different kind of desi mom. About how this would be an opportunity for Sita to create the very generation of even newer, even freer brown girls—if slightly less brown, perhaps—Bhoomija wanted to nurture. "Also," she said, taking the opened bottle out and pouring for the two of them, "your mom doesn't weigh a pound more than she did when she got married, I'd bet. Who says this'll be my last chance to wear this?"

"She doesn't weigh a pound more than the day she got divorced, that's at least true," Pierre said, putting his arms around her, or rather through her bent elbows to drink deep with his wife in his arms. "You can't stress about this stuff, Sit. Just get dressed so we can go and watch the parade." He pulled his arms through, releasing her, and raised his glass and his eyebrows to Nenn. She felt dismissed; she took the gold spangle and the satin and she went. From the bedroom window, she could hear the town's premiere jazz band, out of tune and out of sync. They'd descended from the hilltop and were making their way to the harbor.

Pierre led them to the crowd, pushed his way through to where the people thronged the most closely, and though there were shoulder lengths between them, Sita felt her breath turn to gasps behind the orni she'd wrapped, non-canonically, around her mouth and nose. Pierre wore Nenn in lieu of a pocket square and sheltered him with his palm. Shelter me, Sita wanted to tell him. But Pierre's hand was on the stomach that was no longer her stomach, sheltering whoever resided inside. She wasn't showing yet; he had to use his imagination. Sita herself preferred to imagine the unused space as empty and found it less difficult than she'd been led to believe. She'd craved so many things for so many months and now: nothing. She made a show of serving dinner every night, but hers was food she'd pushed around her plate for three days until the smell would have undone the ruse. She'd felt the sun on her face at midnight and the dark on her face at noon and now, the sky was the grey of the sky out of a school bus window. Somehow the fetus was keeping everything at bay.

Here were Pierre's colleagues, all in a row, the men in suits, as always, as though tradition ran only in women's blood. Their families. The women had their hair in braids pinned against their face, frizzed but intricate, though Mona, who'd laughed so much when they'd gone hiking—not at her but at the lovely weather, the clean air, the katydid calls of the birds Sita was fairly sure weren't actually katydids—wore a plain green hijab to match her bunad, and Sita wished she would have embroidered it with flowers to make the match perfect. She was overwhelmingly, breathtakingly pregnant: her own planet, and Sita thought that next year, the bunad-clad offspring would be Mona's moon. Her own fetus would wear a bunad, too, maybe, she realized, and the thought was enough to make her blink, and then she found herself considering her options for a mid-day, side-of-the-road vomit.

"Lovely dress," said Mona.

Sita nodded and turned to Pierre, or turned, rather, to find he'd wandered off, and walked as quickly as she could to find him without moving any unnecessary parts of her body. "I need to go," she said. His face was blank for a moment, and then she looked at her belly button and back up again, and he took her face with both hands—Nenn lifted his own paws up to shield his eyes—and kissed her on the forehead and took them home.

The walk home was enough to calm her, but Pierre insisted on unwrapping her himself, in pushing open each safety pin as though it was all that held her bones together, on kicking her wet clothes into the corner and laying her upon the bed and making tiny, and then ever larger, circles with his fingertips upon her stomach. "It's the first time," he said. Sita had been following his fingers, and she couldn't draw her eyes away, she realized, or her mind, and she couldn't pin his words onto meanings, his signifiers onto—she didn't know. She closed her eyes and found his fingers still circling, still in tune with the rise and fall of her breath. "The first time he's made us leave early," Pierre said, and he sounded glad and she couldn't imagine why.

She wanted to argue—it would be a girl, surely—but she couldn't speak, and then, when she thought she might be on the verge of something, she slipped into sleep.

*

The next morning the rain carried on, gently. It felt to Sita as though it was unsure of its welcome, and so she was glad to go out, and join it, and felt ready to venture a bit farther than she had. She considered the mountain—she didn't have shoes fit for climbing but it might be nice at the base—but didn't want to pass the health clinic. Pierre had asked her to go in for a visit, had scheduled a meeting with a doctor and in fact went to it, alone, and came back with a bottle of vitamins she pointed out were full of fish oil. The fetus was inside of her, and she was here, where nothing could ever happen, and that was all she could do, the extent of what she could handle.

Her father would chuckle at her intransigence, regret filling his shelves with books on Gandhi, that quack, that were more exciting than the medical journals he pored over in the evenings, ripping out articles he wanted to save and slipping them inside a trapper keeper. And he was glad she was here; they'd encouraged her, her parents, to claim her cosseted destiny, to live her life in a country that was as good as the one they'd promised for her. Sometimes she thought she'd left a shadow Sita in her place, undergoing the torments of capture and release, and sometimes she wondered if Bhoomija was that shadow Sita, but, after all, Bhoomija was never the shadow. And Bhoomija'd never read Tulsidas; though they laughed at being name twins when they were little, Sita knew the most she'd researched for her doomed Ayodhya project, her inaugural Shakti Mag exposé on what had been kept from them, was Nina Paley. But if Bhoomija was real, then was Sita herself the shadow?

Past the pub she turned onto a road she'd avoided specifically because she knew where it led, but today the stave church was empty and no one sang. She unwrapped her scarf and used it to dry her face, and as she wound it round again she thought of Gadhimai, of wood set aflame to send earthly voices higher. Today was a festival that yielded no nostalgia: her parents hadn't observed this Saptami. She'd started to pray to Ganga on her own when she moved to the city and the wind from the lake made its presence known, whipping her curtains round her toes as she slept in the summer, bringing sand to the baby hairs she tried to ignore as she took Lake Shore down to the Loop—as she found herself returning to Lake Shore, no matter how important her meeting might be, how much time it would take to smooth herself into a woman before nine o'clock.

They'd skipped oaths, and sometimes Sita wished she could go back and sit Pierre down to wait, down on the plush red couch

Sita and her roommate, Micah, had inherited from the previous tenants and slip on the first video, the one she'd watched with her parents again and again. A trio of eternal optimists, they'd always started from the beginning, hoping they'd find time enough to sit still until the end of the epic, but even when time looked as though it might stand still for Sita, for the entire country, for Bhoomija—even then she hadn't come home to watch it, for, after all, her parents had been busier than ever, wrapped in plastic, called in to the hospital day and night. And so while she knew the story in its entirety, while at night, and at puja, they'd go forward, pausing only where everyone paused, with Arjuna pausing—she knew the beginning of the epic best, and the beginning was Ganga, extracting a vow from Shantanu.

Once Pierre came home she poured the rest of the wine into their glasses. Before he kissed her face he ran his arms across the plane between her hips. After he talked about work, he told her about an island his colleagues explained was nearby, where next summer, they could take the ferry, and take the baby, and sit on the pebbled beach and swim and watch the village from afar, as though it were in a storybook.

Sita wondered if her lips were stained, if it counteracted the measured lightness of her tone when she asked, "Pierre? Would you promise?"

He cupped her hip. "Promise what?"

"Promise ... not to question anything. Anything I do."

Or else, Ganga had told Shantanu, I'll be gone. But Sita had no way of saying so, no mode but the ferry to who-knew-where to follow through.

He took her head in his other hand and pulled her close, so close she had to set her glass down or it would shatter. So tightly she knew she would have a headache in the morning, and a mark on her hip that would take two days to fade. He kissed her softly and said, "I'll fetch you laitue rapunzel if you ask. Though, Sita, here it may be rotten by the time it arrives." He kissed her roughly then, and he thought her hands on his chest, stopping him, were part of it, and pulled at her wrists, but then he saw, and instead of dropping them he said, "I promise," softly, barely loud enough to be heard over the visiting rain, over her trembling heart, and it had to be enough.

*

On Christmas Eve, Sita awoke five minutes before midnight, soaked through with feverish, milky sweat. The baby was alive, but Pierre had taken it to Paris. He'd balked at leaving her, but she had Nenn, and now that the laws had changed they wouldn't share a passport for years, hers keeping her safely in the village. Well. She might take a boat south, or out to the islands. But the foghorn had been silent since they left and would stay that way until, she assumed, she least expected it.

They'd hung lights from the trees, and though Sita could feel her damp clothes freezing around her she found she could advance a step or two at a time without gasping in fear at the lack of a toehold. Past the shuttered shops, almost at the water, she fell and felt her sleeves crack, but, in the quiet and the dark, nothing interior felt broken.

It was easier to crawl home. Lars couldn't crawl yet—could barely smile—but Sita tucked her reflectors into her pockets, and the ice on her gloved palms achieved an unexpected friction with the ice on the street, and Sita thought about that: unexpected friction. When she'd come back from her semester abroad, she'd moved into the rented room of a girl off to Senegal for the spring, and though her housemates were perfectly civil—nursing students she imagined, hoped, were now being feted by their hometowns—Bhoomija had suggested not forging ties. It was the perfect time, she'd continued, to bring back men without pause. Sita found that the easiest time to do so was when the men were already in her living room: the health sciences students were constantly in her living room, drinking their way through the weekend, bopping to music even she understood wouldn't be cool after graduation, trying to score a pretty nurse but, failing that, a pretty nurse's housemate. The problem with pre-meds—and they were always pre-meds, the boys who had the confidence to flirt with a stranger—was that they always knew someone else Indian. How could they compliment her when that other girl, the one with hair just as long and silken, eyes just as deep, lips just as luscious, was a curve-wrecking thorn in their side? Anthropology, they'd repeat, your parents must be cool.

After a few weekends of this she wondered if the hangovers were worth it. Her Monday 8 a.m. seminar on kinship structures was sparsely attended on the best of weeks, and the day after Valentine's Day she found herself at the seminar table alone—five minutes early, no line for coffee, but surely the professor would show up soon? Three minutes later Micah Steinman slid in, leaned his skateboard against the back wall, and sat down across from her. "You look rough," he commented.

She'd thanked him, sighed. They'd had most electives together sophomore year, but had gone their separate ways in the fall—if she remembered correctly Micah had gone to Peru and learned Quechua there. "Micah," she said, because if the instructor was sick or something she might as well get something out of this hour, "are your parents cool?" Or did a fondness for offspring who could contribute towards the deciphering of human culture only render coolness on hers?

"Uh, sure," he'd said, and she soon found that he was right. He pulled out his cell to reveal the virtual classroom update everyone else had checked from their beds—yup, he was sick—and laughed. "We should check our phones more often," he said, and invited her back to his for pancakes. It turned out Micah lived with his parents in a rowhouse she'd assumed, upon previous glance, was subdivided into student apartments. The kitchen was the size of her first-grade classroom, with a farmhouse vibe— no island, but rather a massive, rough-hewn table and several mismatched chairs—and two very present adults listening to NPR and drinking coffee that smelled much better than the one she held in her hands and now wished she'd jettisoned in the frigid classroom.

She unwrapped her red scarf as Micah made introductions; he had a different last name than either of his parents, which she pushed to the side as a puzzle to be sorted later, and his mother was a doctor with the same sub-specialization as her own and re-marked on this by referring to a paper Sita's mother had been quoted in and which Sita had not heard of, much less read. His father was a professor she'd wanted to take a class with freshman year but couldn't get into (she had been pleasantly surprised by her back-up gen ed, a deep dive into the Ottoman Empire—those chintamani silks!). When his mother left, his father joined them, pouring them both coffees and gesturing for her to join him at the table. "We could help, but Micah likes to show off a bit with pancakes."

By the time the pancakes arrived, light as Turkish towels, with swirled honey and butter dripping down the sides, she'd found a senior thesis advisor. When she explained that she wanted to write about shame in Eastern and Western culture, he'd laughed such a full laugh she was ready to drop out of school. "No, no," he said, looking at her bottom eyelids, "I'm just thinking about how much I'd like to poach you."

If she took summer classes instead of interning at the ad agencies she'd been writing to, using her best friend's address so it looked like she already lived in New York, she could write an honors thesis and still graduate on time. She moved out of her sublet and into a house full of seniors who'd decided to chill until their lease ran out—though they'd have been equally as sanguine about any amorous adventures, her basement room full of spiders didn't inspire lust, and anyways, she was too busy. Her professor had told her to spend the summer narrowing her focus to one place, one time, and when she explained that what she wanted to do was understand the topic as a whole he invited her to family dinner, where he started in on a lecture she realized, based on Micah's rolled eyes, he'd given before. The only way to understand concepts, he told her, was to understand examples. The only way to compare, he went on, anticipating her next question, was to wholly inhabit the present and work from within it.

The professor's wife asked her if she wanted coffee, which Sita had seen people order after dinner in movies but didn't understand, given her admittedly rudimentary knowledge of caffeine. She said yes, and the wife poured out a cup and put a record on and began talking to the boys about the news the way doctors did, furious about a woman who'd been forced by her family onto never-ending life support, and Sita realized she hadn't called her parents in weeks. Once she was sure Micah wasn't listening she confessed to her professor that she didn't quite understand how to work from within the present. The world, today, was too shameful to think about at any length.

"Well, how does shame work for you?" he asked.

"Yes, but—" she realized she couldn't quite bear to say what she wanted to say, that though she'd spent the entirety of last semester sleeping with strangers in an attempt to wholly inhabit the present, she knew she would never be here now in the way he seemed to suggest she required, for she was always also that other Indian girl, who also inhabited the now, and whose experience of shame seemed to require her. Who did Micah's shame require, or did he not feel any?

"Just pick a place and go from there," he said. "If you want to focus on the Quechua, I'm sure Micah could give you pointers."

In her division of the world into halves she'd forgotten about the non-Spanish-speaking peoples of Latin America, and Micah, for his part, was happy not to educate her. Instead, there were further dinners, where unless Micah prepared something they simply held vegetables up to the fire as though they were girl scouts, and laid out pretentious loaves of bread and dribbly cheeses and the sort of cheap and cheerful wine she'd become accustomated to drinking out of solo cups. They weren't ashamed of it, she realized one day, and all of a sudden she'd figured out how to write a paper that he would love while also pretending to retain, as she was for some reason desperate to, some modicum of interest in her original idea.

"I don't think I'm going to New York after graduation," she told the professor one day as they watched Micah julienne carrots.

"I didn't realize you wanted to," he said. "I thought you wanted to go to grad school. Though they have grad schools in New York, technically."

"I sort of promised my friend I would," she explained. "She's already there. She needs a roommate to make rent on her studio." Bhoomija had been forced to give back an advance for her biggest commission yet—a 21st-century feminist update of the Ramayana ghostwritten for the latest Bollywood star to cross over—when she'd insisted on referring to the agni pariksha as—Sita groaned, remembering—one of Rama's attempted murders.

He shrugged. "You have to live your own life."

She wished he could have gone with her when she went up to the city—meaning Chicago—to do her interviews with shoppers on Devon. By April of her senior year she was prouder of "Unashamed in the Kitchen: How a MetLife Ad Gave Immigrant Wives the Freedom to Call Home" than of anything else she'd ever done, but she knew she wouldn't want to do it again. It was the professor's wife who sorted things, in the end, suggesting she parlay her hard-earned knowledge into a feigned enthusiasm for working at MetLife, spend her hard-earned salary on half of the sublet Micah'd found near his next project: culinary school. The professor groaned, but when she got an interview, he took her out for coffee and placed on the table, so poorly wrapped she knew he'd done it himself, a copy of *A History of Knitcraft*. "You're always clicking away, so ..." When she got the job offer, she gave him a scarf in university colors, an Aran moss stitch, twelve diamonds long. When her parents finally met him, at the post-graduation drinks reception where they held fluted cups they had no intention of drinking, she saw that he was wearing it, and she saw that her parents recognized her work around his neck, and then: then she felt shame.

*

When Sita opened her eyes, it was still dark, but the lights strung up between the trees along the street made her think of Ayodhya, so many years ago. The light in her face made her blink. Behind it was a ruddy-faced woman wearing a thermal neon Marius-print hijab. "Merry Christmas," she said. She held a flask up to Sita's lips, and it had been filled with gin, and Sita felt her fingers and toes proclaiming their existence. "Do you need a hand up?"

She found she didn't, for the woman was willing to wait. Besides the lights, the road was quiet so that the sound of the waves lapping along the pier helped her steady her breath. She reached out for more gin and was given the flask.

"You're welcome to join us at the cabin," said the woman. After a minute she added, "We told Pierre I'd fetch you but as you're all right . . . ?"

Oh, yes. Mona the surfer, Morten's partner. Sita had thought she might reach out again, despite her own rudeness—expected it, frankly: the diaspora connection. But Mona had a life's worth of a family here, a mosque's worth, and maybe it was clear that an American of some other, random, brownness would be superfluous. Unlike Morten, she hadn't studied in America, and when Sita had told her, that night at the pier, that she'd been a copywriter back home, Mona had thought she meant writer, and kept asking her for stories. Sita hadn't known what to say; she wasn't Bhoomija. "I'm all right," she agreed.

"Still, if you'd like?"

Sita shook her head, and Mona didn't press. They walked together until the corner where Mona had parked, and before she could cross the road, Mona said, "You know, we can hike together more than once a year."

Sita was drawing the kitchen curtains against the aurora when her phone lit up too brightly to ignore. "We'll come home," said Pierre. She'd gotten so used to leaning the device against a bowl so his mother, Hang, and Lars could make faces at one another that she stared at it until Pierre's voice came out again. "Sita? There aren't flights today, but if we leave tomorrow, we can be home by the day after."

"It's not been two weeks yet," she pointed out. There was a flare-up on the continent; they wouldn't be allowed on a plane. "How are they getting on, your mom and the baby?"

"Morten called me, said his parents saw you fall over out their front window," he said. "Were you drunk?"

"Is he speaking French with her?" she asked.

"What?" he said. "Look, I can keep our original ticket, but you need to answer your phone when I call. And stay sober. And stay inside, I think."

"I mean, how do they communicate?"

"He gurgles, she speaks French, of course. Sita. I need you to promise."

"Of course," she said.

Bhoomija would have said yes to Mona. When Bhoomija had come to visit Sita the autumn after graduation, she came unannounced, and Micah buzzed her in the way he would anyone, and was surprised when, a minute later, she knocked on their door. Sita came out of her bedroom to find her appraising Micah and nodding. "I can see how your dad might be kind of hot." She spotted Sita, dropped her duffel and her backpack, and ran into her arms. "Oh, god, I'm so glad you're here. We have so much work to do."

"I'm glad you're here, too?"

They had to stay in the city; she didn't want her parents to know she was nearby when it was only Sita she wanted to see. The problem was after that business with her advance, she was being blacklisted. The real way forward, she explained, was to found something, and instead of spending half her life hustling for commissions she'd spend half her life marketing the zine, bringing all of them forward at once. She could figure out the tech stuff but there was no time left after that to do the cold calls, the e-mails, the accounting to make sure they could tell their sponsors what went to site maintenance, how much actually reached the WOC writers and illustrators she planned to feature. "White women are out there arguing whether or not real women have curves and we call bullshit," Bhoomija explained to Micah, as Sita checked Bhoomija's bag to see if she'd packed a toothbrush or whether they needed to make a trip to the Walgreens or what. "We care about breaking free of the gaze altogether, whether white aunties' or brown uncles', and that's what this is. *Shakti*: a new age zine to give us back our eyes, not our curves or lack thereof. So you'd better be ready to break your lease."

Later that night they were head to head on the mattress, and

Sita denied sleeping with father or son. It wasn't them, she said. The whole family was incidental. She was just fine with her job, with her studio, with monthly rides on the commuter rail to the burbs for a weekend of daal chaawal and mandir, three more rows on the lattice-stitch coverlet she was hoping would grace her parents' horrible leather sofa by their anniversary, Sa Re Ga Ma Pa Little Champs. Did she have to show how proud she was by leaving everything? She just didn't have the same dreams. She didn't have dreams at all.

"What a waste," said Micah, as she closed the door on Bhoomija Monday morning, on the whole thing. Of what, she'd wanted to ask, but in the end she didn't.

"Do you think I should move to New York and start a zine?" Sita asked the professor that afternoon, on the phone from her cubicle now that she had nothing to do with campus.

"Of course I do. I'm embarrassed whenever my students graduate into a job that requires a button-down shirt. But do you?"

She shrugged, then spoke. "Maybe. It's scary to see her doing everything we talked about doing. She's leaving me behind."

"Sounds like she's trying not to."

When they got back to the apartment, it was late, and the streets were loud: they'd forgotten about Halloween. Bhoomija was sitting on the doorstep, holding her bags. "Thank god you're home," she said. "I desperately need to pee." After she came out of the bathroom she forced them to dress in costume, rolling her eyes at Sita's out-of-fashion lengha, and when Micah rolled his eyes, too, linked hands with him as they made their way down to Rush and Division. Sita kept having to run to avoid being left behind.

"I've been thinking about your invitation," Sita said, once they were at the bar, but Micah had gotten shots for them, and Sita wondered if she was really going to do it. When she came back from the fetid bar bathroom, Bhoomija and Micah were making out on the dance floor, and she perched back on her stool and tried not to watch them. She considered bringing out the half-made pair of mittens she'd started on the train: simple, close checks, in navy mohair, but there was a group in undone ties on the other side of the room, and one of them was looking appreciatively at her midriff, so instead she sat up straighter, and smiled.

The first time she left the baby with Nenn was when the sun rose. Lars was an incurious child. He contained, she'd hoped, some glimmer of suppressed light that would burst forth on Makar midday with the sun's reappearance. A week earlier, as night stood ramrod straight through everything, Pierre had ruined Sita's plans for an annaprashan by breaking the gallette des rois she'd baked him into tiny pieces and placing them alternately on the tongues of his baby and his pet. For two days after, Sita had left the lights off in the kitchen whenever she ate, until it became clear Lars cared not one whit about her porridge or her onions. He was content to sit on the counter, staring at the sky, until Nenn came home. Then she'd place him on the floor, relieved: Nenn would mime akar bakar bambe bo with him until both were reduced to gleeful fits. So on Makar morning, Sita mashed sesame snaps with abandon, attempting to reverse engineer til ke laddoo, and when a tiny hand outstretched itself in the corner of her eye, she assumed it was Nenn home early—he kept unsteady hours, an eerie if benign ghost keeping corner—until the soft, nail-free nubs hit her fingertips, and she jumped. "Tujhe bhi khaana hain, phir?" she asked, guiding the baby's fair fingers to his mouth. For a moment, as he sucked on seed and sugar, she imagined he understood her; a moment was enough to reignite her dreams of all-day hikes filled with antakshari and un-eavesdroppable gossip. Then his nose crinkled at the sweet, or perhaps at the rough, and tears filled his eyes; she bared him her breast and wondered if she'd been such a drag.

By the time Nenn gave her his wide-eyed nodded greeting, she'd brushed her abortive baking attempts into the trash and was staring at Lars, splayed out on the counter, full and fast asleep, counting the stitches she'd need to knit him long johns. Nenn had been wearing two scarves at once, one purple and the other greige, and was unwinding them from above his eyes and below his chin, and after hanging them on their hooks he hopped up beside her and tickled Lars in the soft folds beneath his chin; nary a stir. It looked like the sun would pass them by, today, its reappearance to be marked only by the smug grunts of the shrimp vendors counting their post-lunch gains. She wanted to shrug at Nenn, but the thought of no reply made her heart still. There was only this to do: stare at the lumpen boy before them and let the light slip away unseen.

The foghorn: it made her jump, and even this did not wake Lars. During the dark days, she'd not bothered to keep Lars on a schedule; if Pierre liked to wake him when he returned from work and read to him, news from all over the world but especially from town in which they had both been working when they met, it was hardly her business. And so now the only way to wake him would be with cheer, with song, with inducements Sita could hardly—would hardly—summon up before seeing the tiniest bit of proof that they were not trapped in an everlasting darkness. If only Nenn would speak to her again, she could dispatch him, and he could report back.

Or she could report back. Another child—the child she imagined for herself when she woke, startled by the shattering of a fallen icicle on the doorstep, and pulled him towards her—would wonder, upon waking, where she had gone.

"An hour," she told him, and then she was out of the house so quickly she had nothing wrapped to her at all.

She had to head away from town, of course; if she were seen, Lars would be seized and Pierre would abandon her to some glum hinterland prison. But from the top of the hill she could look down on the boats and the fjord beyond, and the islands that seemed to float in the sky instead of in the sea. And when the sun breached the horizon she raised her arms in greeting, and couldn't stop herself: she sunk down, prostrate, and kissed the ice and shed tears upon it, and raised her arms towards the sun once again. Here, she was nothing but a body casting shadows. And perhaps Lars was her son, truly, for in that moment she thought nothing of the lives she wasn't living.

The next day she prolonged Nenn's night still further, and by third day she understood that whatever else he spoke about with Pierre, on this he'd stay mum. Wasn't he a brother, by proxy if not by birth? Wasn't he more than capable of sustaining life? Wasn't she—taking a creature into her heart—assimilating as they all wanted?

As the sun tested its welcome, rays brighter and stronger than in the winters of her childhood, Pierre grew merry. The ship heralded by the horn had brought a carnival to town until the month's end, and on its last evening she was to have Lars and herself prepared for a night out. "We can get his chart read, just like you wanted," he offered, eating, it was true, potatoes she didn't remember undersalting, and instead of giving him a sidelong glance and a punch on the arm she merely raised her eyebrows and went back to her knitting. When Lars refused his proffered bite, she merely let her lips quiver. How much smaller he loomed that week, her jeevansathi, this man she'd stretched out over her heart and mind and soul so fearlessly, so heedlessly. What did he know of Lars, of her, of Nenn, of anything beyond the world he'd kept for himself? What did he know of the sun in the winter and the way the ice tasted of a candle blown out in one swift breath?

*

The night before the new moon, as Nenn taught Lars to find his face in the mirror, Pierre mixed Sita an old fashioned. The drink she'd loved before the baby's arrival now tasted liked raw jackfruit; she decided to take small bites of the unsalted potato she'd mashed Lars in between each sip. Pierre was drinking hard liquor, too—recounting his discussion with Morten that day about grandmothers. Morten's mother had set up a bassinet in the corner of the fishmongers', while Pierre's mother, Hang, was grouching about their lack of Easter visit this year; Pierre wanted to save money in case they had to leave here, too, when the violence of the new war spread. The American officers had arrived already, on the same ferries as the circus showmen and their animals. He was calling Nenn "champ" again and suggesting he tell Lars all about the ferry, which made Sita cough up a cursed sip. Perhaps she had understood that Nenn had come from somewhere—she had to have known—but as Pierre chronicled Nenn's abandonment by the very carnival they'd attend tomorrow, and his refuge-taking in the woods behind a coworker's home until Pierre noticed him and expressed interest, Sita felt shame and intoxication mingle within her.

There was sun enough for everyone now; the moon shied away, and the night would be solemn underneath the canopy of carnival lights and blazing borealis, but there would have been

time, she knew, to take Lars with her. But her good intentions
were overlaid by a hung-over headache and a creeping anxiety
that had her determined to stop at the clinic pharmacy to pre-
vent any further children from gracing their home—perhaps
they might forget to mention her visit to Pierre the next time
he stopped in for aspirin, but they'd never forget to mention the
baby. So she was alone when she heard the snake charmer's
music: sinewy rather than sinuous, but all notes accounted for,
completely unmistakable. By the time she'd descended to the carnival on the green foot of the hill, it was almost buried beneath
calls to food, to darts, to any manner of games that, upon win-
ning, would find one in bemused ownership of a goldfish—almost.

It would have been better buried; the fakir, when spotted, had
long blonde locs and an unattended wicker basket lined, presumably, for the comfort of gathered coins rather than Indian ser-
pents. She let herself scoff aloud and continued her search for the
astrologer who, it was true, accepted money to speak of the past,
as well. The fakir remembered Nenn vaguely but confidently: he
hadn't been a part of the carnival so much as a barnacle, he re-
counted, and when he was fully grown he ate enough to warrant
what had come to him—not, he assured her, that anyone wanted
him to starve to death. They'd always trusted in the kindness of
strangers: after all, here she was. On her walk home, Sita ventured

into the ice to vomit and tried her best not to slip into the patch she'd defiled. The day's fasting rendered it slick, her throat sour.

It was time for onions; no, she reminded herself, time for puja, and if hers was not a religion where souls could be prayed for, well, she was hardly a model parishioner. All this time there had been a body in her house who understood what it meant to be enrobed by luck and trapped by it. The gritted path sent spray into her eyes as it propelled her and so until she was at the door she did not see Nenn outside of it, his hands, his mouth, his tongue: bloody.

She had always felt watched, a flailing light against a starry sky, but in this moment she could only see, and only straight in front of her. Pierre would have been cruel, had he tried to replicate her movements: summers near Gadhimai had shown her just how to snap an animal's neck so it severed in one movement, how to toss it on its forehead to make sure it was dead. But Sita was cruel in her killing, too, for as she flicked her wrist Nenn's bones tangled up in her scarf. In the extra second her clumsiness added to Nenn's life, Sita could see the animal she'd thought had spilled her son's blood was covered, too, with ripped snakeskin. Nenn's eyes were amavas-dark, amavas-dim, but as he died his head was cushioned, and Sita couldn't spare a moment to discern her feelings, whether her error made her sweet or foolish. If Lars had been left to breathe, all of her spare moments were his.

The house greeted her with silence. She left on her shoes. And then: her son, on the counter, wrapping as best he could a silenced, throat-bit snake around his neck. She heard herself exhale, felt her fingers thaw. And then she sank to the floor and began to chant.

*

Night and day were bifurcated now, neatly, and when it rained, as it often did, the clouds took the moon's cue and left at dawn. Pierre slept with Lars, his hands ludicrously large against the soft skin of her son's stomach. She left now, as soon as she knew her feet would be visible in the shade cast by her umbrella, and crossed the town and the hill and went straight to the mountains. By the time she returned something was always left for her, simmering on the stove, something full of cream and butter and wine and it felt like nothing so much as stumbling upon a witch's cabin.

She kept her phone close, though he never called; daily, she was supposed to call a friend, perhaps a former coworker from the city, anyone she liked, Pierre said in his magnanimous way. The internet in the mountains was fast, and the pixels on the screen tiny and sharp—not like eyes at all, she knew, but it hurt to look at them, and for what? She knew how she would vote, fifty years into the future; she knew what the weather was, today. She knew the shankh cry of the military planes amassing were here to mourn the crashed American plane, dead countrymen she'd never known though they had been so close. Beyond that were mere facts: names of constellations grown more inaccessible with each lengthening day, incoming ships' previous ports of call, so she might guess what it was safe to dream of, the actual and scientific composition of the moon.

If they separated, she'd hardly see him less: Pierre kept Lars close now, protected and protector. She'd return to the city, reapply for her job, make muffled jokes in her interview about her dreams of romance and the cold, sharp slap of reality. She would take nothing from this house but for a bag full of yarn, for today, she celebrated Holi by unraveling each tiny scarf, the colors bursts of unmade mischief against her skin. It was hardly traditional, but it was a comfort against the unspoken tradition she knew she had started: each year, her family would grow older, and weaker, and more silent. Each year, looking north, she would remember that she had wandered so gracelessly into this shanti, shanti, shantih.

PART TWO

5

She was hungry. Sita felt as one would who had lived on land, and now that the sea had risen lived underwater, with the fruits, now, soggy and flavorless and cold to the touch. Lars' expulsion from her body had seemed a discrete act, but the blood was staunched and still, and again, she felt herself pulled inside out. Hang had taken to calling her from France almost daily, demanding photographs. And there he would be, unexpectedly writhing on the tiny screen of Sita's phone, and there, too, beside it, constantly doubling, and in response she pushed as much food into herself as she could to make up for the lack of one satisfying crunch. Pierre—designated buyer of groceries during official lockdown periods, halfhearted buyer of groceries now—did what he could, he said; often, after she emerged from the bath in the evening, she'd find him and Lars and the newly-purchased, thick-wheeled stroller gone for an evening wander around the aisles. Or down the pier, perhaps; tonight he slipped off his shoes by the door and hung next to them, neatly, a wrung-out pair of bright blue swim shorts. Lars—and this was unheard of—was crying.

It had been almost a year since she'd done what she could, wrapped the baby up in a yellow rose-stitch cashmere blanket and a matching hat she'd knit points into to resemble a crown, and though she was free to take him from the clinic bed to his crib whenever she wished, she presumed, her Janmashtmi scene had felt almost real. And she'd held the bottle out to Pierre and he, the bottle to Lars' freckle of a mouth. Since just before Holi, when Pierre had abruptly begun what his office had deemed paternity leave, the crib had been abandoned; Lars slept between them in the same manner Sita had slept between her parents even long after the purchase of a purple coverlet for the bed in the spare room, of a purple dupatta re-hemmed to be princess curtains to make it a childhood bedroom. On the National Day of this foreign nation, Pierre had gone out in the evening— "Morten's party," he'd said, as though she could put names to the same four faces alternating across his myriad co-workers—and Sita had curved her arm into a shepherd's crook to stop her log of a son from rolling until he fell, and then he had rolled, but towards her, and though by the time the sun took firm hold of its place in the sky Lars would be almost a year old, he'd found her breast again. And without Pierre's wary witness, she'd given herself over to the feast.

And now there was nothing, just the sea and the sky all one enveloping hue, no night to tell her changeling child to stop, stop, please, stop eating. There could be no more solitary mountain treks; instead, they sat together on the living room floor in a pulling embrace while Pierre sat on the couch and tried to coax a smile from a baby who'd never been more determined to do anything in his short life than this twisted turning back of time. There was a limit to the onions one could eat while constantly touching a baby's face and so she began to eat the pillowy bread Pierre kept for Lars' breakfast eggy soldiers, and he was touched for awhile—see, they all ate bread now, like a family—and he would begin to knead her shoulders and pause at the puffiness of her skin and leave her, unbalanced, to knead Lars' legs instead. In a week the moon would narrow itself to nothing and the dark would depart, and until then she would stay awake to greet it and eat jam, which she'd always hated, even as a child surrounded by sandwiches, dipping her finger in to avoid dishes, detection. And in a week Pierre would depart after each foreshortened night, his leave spent, so when he took the baby now she tried to sleep, and felt her stomach curdle, and started to shake but wouldn't, absolutely wouldn't let Lars back on her breast until the allocated time.

But she must—after an hour Pierre took the baby at his word-less commitment and spent the afternoon, and the next three af-ternoons, swimming. He'd told Sita the story, once, back in their first months together in the city when he'd spent Thursday nights playing 5-a-side and so she'd not dropped out of Knit n' Bitch, of his fourth-grade year, when he was the fastest boy on the swim team. Now slicing through the water seemed to take him forever, and she would stare into Lars' coal-dark eyes and whisper the Gayatri mantra before cursing herself for encourag-ing the sun, hastening her abandonment. Tonight, Pierre said, he would be late, shopping alone: tomorrow was the start of the Ascension holiday and he wanted romaine, he wanted lamb, he wanted whole carts of foods Sita knew wouldn't fill her.

Pierre had moved here to work and yet Sita couldn't remember a time when she'd known him happier than those daily seconds at the door, hanging up his wrung suit, casting his eyes about for his son. As the moon retreated for good she realized there wasn't a pool in the village, just the fjord and, as it opened out into the sea, a meager shore which this spring had been dotted with tiny jellyfish corpses, their clear and purple bodies surprisingly warm to the touch. By the time she remembered to ask, she'd made her way halfway through a stale tin of gingerbread, and as Lars pulled her closer with nails sharper than sharks' teeth she swallowed her anger and she swallowed as many cookies as it took to get a sharp hit of ginger on her tongue. Sometimes he swam in the fjord, but also at the cabin, he responded, and, after a beat, "Morten's. Not a pool, just a lake."

The next day Hang called Pierre just as he was leaving. He came back in and took the phone off his ear to snap a picture and so Sita could hear Hang's comments on her hair and the jawline below. "Maman," Pierre chided, but after he hung up he said, "Why don't you two come out to the cabin with us today? Mona might be there. And you could take a turn swimming."

God, she was starved.

"Sita?" He'd come and sat beside her on the floor, instead of on the drab grey sofa that had been featured in the ad for the house when they'd paid their deposit and onto which she'd thrown a dozen striped baby blankets, and he pulled Lars up from her arms and bounced him on his knee. It wasn't clear who he looked like, his tiny black curls oily and ruffled. When Pierre secured the baby's head in his right palm, he took his left and ran it up and down the top of her spine, bent his fingers round her neck, and when she shivered, he turned his face to her, and it was stone and he said, "I think it'll be good for us."

*

"Vriksh," she whispered to Lars, newly awake in his sling. "Dekho, munna, vriksh." The woods here, on the far side of the mountain, were greener, wetter. When she'd attempted to pull her bathing suit on, her thighs had scoffed, so Sita'd strapped Lars in and begun to wander. Out here, the quiet felt deliberate, but unimposing; it felt like she could join in without giving away anything, and so she let her narration die out. Without her words the air was wet and uninterrupted.

Though it was midday the sun would not be at its brightest until its unending descent. It was too far above them, perhaps, to bestow anything but a soft grey light, and as Sita looked at the slurping, pursed body atop hers she thought of her mother, brows furrowed as she filed their taxes, and so Sita turned her mind to samsara, and then, for what else was there, to her terrible hunger. The forest was full, but these were pine needles, and moss on stones, and birds still too young to fly and their mothers, to and fro, bearing worms. Not that she'd eat a bird. But there were ways of bloodletting, weren't there, that weren't fatal? Blood, surely, tasted.

"Stella?" Morten's voice was built for this place; his nickname for her wound through the shadows and landed at her feet, where she thought to ignore it. Lars loved Morten, she could tell: his rough red beard, his calves like—well, Lars wouldn't know a watermelon. Calves like seven peeled, piled apples. She looked down, but Lars had fallen asleep again, his teeth slid forward to clench around the tips of her nipples; they'd draw blood if she didn't wake him, just for one moment, but then the cry would draw the men in further. As he'd loaded Lars into Morten's car seat this morning,

Sita was reminded yet again that Pierre was, after all, still himself: every step a spring. She could see Lars following along with their guttural vernacular, and then, child secured, Pierre had stepped neatly towards the front and gestured for her to sit and Morten had said, in a cowboy's drawl, "Nice to see ya again." He'd spent a semester at a small college in Georgia and, de Tocqueville or not, he was here to tell her what he'd thought about it.

She wondered if there was another way out, one that would lead her to another side of the lake, maybe, but when she lifted her heel to move, the pain in her breast was sharp and restricting. She slid her nails under the two-toned lips that made her feel, more than anything else, that she existed in this village, in this body, and all she wanted in recompense and recognition was ghee and lime juice and crushed red pepper and garlic and corn that didn't taste of the inside of a birdhouse. As the baby lunged for her other nipple she backed herself further into the trees, slid on her heels, on and on until the leafy canopy brought a new darkness, a welcome stillness.

A gape, in fact. She looked down and found Lars, mouth open, looking up. Not at her. Behind her. She squeezed him as she turned, but there was no one there. An old tree, dark and knotted, thick and full. She took a measured step toward it and tried to see behind it without moving further. The animals she'd come across in this corner of the world weren't small enough to hide behind a tree trunk, but then again, not everything in the woods was native to them. Another step. Still nothing. She looked down at Lars, but he was playing with her hair now, destroying her braid. She looked up, and there they were.

Part of her wanted to stop and take stock, just for a moment, of how beautiful they were: dark pink paisley drops, two together like doves. But she had been so very hungry, and she reached up with both hands and plucked the rose apples and held one to Lars' mouth and let her teeth, her tongue, her throat cling to the juice of each bite, and soon hers was eaten and she looked down at her child and his was done, too, and she thought, for the first time, that perhaps her incomprehensibly clutching child might simply be thirsty.

*

They'd gotten lost, she lied—well, who knew if she'd have been able to find her way back through the woods?—and Morten whistled, impressed, told Pierre she was as resourceful as one of their girls, seeking out shoreline, and she forced her eyes not to roll when Pierre glowed in response, picked Lars up and spun him in a circle around the small grassy beach they'd found their way to, where Lars had examined sticks and she'd worked on a new project—a pair of dark pink baby socks, bee stitch—all afternoon. The lakeshore had curved to the east and though she couldn't see them, she could hear periodic guffaws and splashes and, at one point, smelled sausages. Now they'd come with a boat, and she held her breath as Pierre took Lars on his lap for the gentle ride, let him trail his fingers in the deep, cool green.

"Come tomorrow," said Morten, for her benefit, as he dropped them off, and she nodded. She saw Pierre's sharp, quizzing glance, but didn't respond.

That night she slept deeply, and when she woke, she saw the bed empty beside her, a small circle of milk pooled beneath her chest. She took a deep breath. For a moment she waited, and, then, still—she felt nothing.

As she stripped her t-shirt and the sheets, she opened the window—almost two thousand years ago and a day, if sources Pierre held dear were to be believed, a singular avatar was raised into heaven. States changed. The breeze that entered the house was warm and she went into the kitchen topless and saw Pierre and Lars stirring the eggs with a wooden spoon, and though Pierre's eyes, when he looked up, went first to her pendulous gut and then next to her eyes, he smiled.

She made tea and watched Pierre fill a picnic basket, and by the time Morten's car arrived, the sheets were drying on the line. She'd pushed for a dryer—wouldn't sheets en plein air become unmanageable during the next lockdown? Weren't they bird-feeders for fatal germs?—but when it had come, she found it refused her entreaties, no matter how many times she restarted the cycle, to leave clothes anything but damp. In the winter she'd draped them over the couch; on the porch they would have turned to ice.

The men plunged into the lake—"Don't go so far today, Stella," Morten chided, chuckling—and though she wanted to run she kept her gait steady, for if she fell there went Lars, squashed, and, after all, there was no reason to believe that today, when almost two thousand years ago people were getting on with the realization that no matter how he'd done it, their avatar was gone now, yet the Romans remained, that once they fell they'd spring back to life. In the sling Lars drank from her, but slowly, as though she were fine china. In the trees the baby birds were just slightly more awake, more alert, closer to sounding fully real.

This time, she paused, nay—stopped. "Mumma," whispered Lars.

"Dekho, munna," she whispered back.

If she waited too long, she was sure, they would dematerialize in front of her eyes. Rose apples had been hard to find even in the US. On visits to his parents' home, she would sit with her father at the table, sometimes, as he peeled them—you didn't need to peel them, but with her non-native stomach, in India she peeled everything she couldn't boil or fry—and diced them, slowly, but carefully, a man unused to kitchen tasks. They'd only met Pierre once but Papa'd placed his arm on her shoulder, and squeezed, as Pierre watched her mother make litti and shared, brightly, and so amiably, Hang's recipe for bao. Here she could place the entire fruit between Lars' budding teeth, and as she bit into her own the taste was so clear she forgot her tears.

Morten was due elsewhere for the rest of the long weekend, to his in-laws' home with Mona, where his own child had been ensconced, but as he bade them goodbye that evening he handed Pierre the keys and told them to enjoy. Pierre narrated their plans to Lars as he put their lunch leftovers into a stew: a rented car, and wouldn't he enjoy those olives they'd picked out together last week, and wouldn't Lars enjoy sleeping in a new bed for a night? With Papa and Maman, yes, of course, Doudou. He let Lars run his fingers under the open tap, and Lars' cheeks quivered. "L'eau, l'eau!"

"He said my name today," she said, though he hadn't; he'd just hissed. "When we were walking."

Pierre looked up. "That's wonderful, Sita."

She didn't know what to say next, what she wanted to hear. She went to pack her things. Tomorrow, she vowed, she would sit with the tree day and sun-drenched night and then until day again and watch them grow. The trick, she thought, was to stay close.

The water was as cold as promised but Pierre and Lars stood on
the shore, clapping for her, and so she went a step farther, a step
deeper. Underneath her feet she felt the rough sand rise and fall;
she felt the thick strips of seaweed twist around her ankles and
then around her unclothed ass. The second night of uninterrupted sleep made her relatively sure she wouldn't slip. She considered turning around and then felt the tip of her braid take in
water. She held her breath and bent her knees to bring the water
over her nipples quickly, and then tilted her head back to let
the water have all of her hair, let the sun shine its muted light
straight down on all of her face.

By the time she rejoined them, Pierre and Lars had set up the
red-checked blanket and poured two cups of cheap champagne
and a milky bottle, set the sour strawberries out and the tasteless
olives without garlic nestled where pits had once been, and a long

crusty loaf that she no longer, she realized, felt drawn to. Pierre squeezed cheese out of tube onto Lars' tongue and looked at her and laughed. "I'm going to miss you both next week."

She watched until she was sure Lars wouldn't choke on the cheese and then she nodded.

"I'll come back at lunchtime to see you," he said.

She was shivering and it had been for his amusement and she drew her towel around her shoulders more tightly. "We'll be fine."

"I know," he said, quickly.

Lars was squeezing the cheese paste onto the sand and she watched him do it.

"I've asked Morten to stop by every so often," Pierre said. "He's off on his parental quota now all summer, with Signe. Lars gets on with her, you know. We took them to Baby Sing."

"Baby Sing," she repeated, and stood up. "I need to go for a walk. You've got him?"

By the time the mother birds had finished feeding and the sun's warmth began to hover, its rays to cast in sepia, the tree hadn't done anything beyond yield, as she was beginning to expect, its two sweet fruits upon arrival. Her breasts began to feel tight and her ribcage to lose hope of any nocturnal reunion with her spawn, for whom she knew she should rightfully have saved one of the rose apples. She hadn't dressed and so when her nipples began to leak she pressed her towel against them and wondered if Pierre had left Lars asleep in Signe's crib to continue swimming. No, he wouldn't. Perhaps if he had been able to think of a way to carry it to the beach, but Pierre was lithe, his musculature mostly for show.

The bright night made it easy to stay away, to watch the bare branch on the strange tree remain bare, remain open, and waiting, and willing. Then she could hear owls and wondered if time had stopped, and then she could hear her husband's voice and her son's tears and blinked, and by the time Lars fairly leapt from his father's arms to drain her, she could see two tiny pink fruits shining out of the corner of her eye.

The next day she awoke to an empty bed, but in the kitchen Pierre was pacing, and when he saw her he nodded and headed straight for the door. "Morten is coming at nine," he said. "He'll have Signe. Be dressed and ready."

She dressed Lars for the woods, in his new pink socks, but he turned up sans car and told her to pack a blanket so Lars could sleep outside in his stroller if they stopped for a beer. Morten paused. "Are you allowed to drink?"

She couldn't understand what Pierre had told him, nor did she have any intention of pushing the tank-sized stroller Pierre had insisted upon—she could see why now, with Signe asleep in a matching model—to the village pub, or the village hot dog stand, or the row of shops she'd not been in since, well, since. "Let's go to the cabin," she said, not sure if she was misgendering the word for cabin.

"Not enough car seats," he said, shrugging. "Have you met mine, yet? Isn't she a beauty?"

She was very much not a beauty—Signe looked like an under-toasted marshmallow swaddled in at least four layers beyond what was necessary for the glorious weather—but Sita cooed and considered her options. If she managed to be rid of him she wouldn't be able to leave the house at all, and Lars was already trying to peel her blouse off. If she mismanaged an attempt to be rid of him she might never find her way to the woods again. "I'll grab a blanket," she said, "and we'll stop by the shops and see if there are any seats in."

*

Occasionally, she tried to ask Morten where his girlfriend was. It had to do with her mosque commitments to welcoming the new refugees as she would have wished to have been herself wel-comed, but it also had something to do with summer, her disap-pearance: changing work schedules and cruise ships and surfing waves. Even though Morten always switched to English the sec-ond she made a grammatical mistake or used a proper term when slang would be common, she couldn't make heads or tails of the mysterious Mona, who'd wanted to be her friend once, she'd thought. At the end of this he would pitch his voice lower. "Don't worry, Stella. She's not the jealous type."

More than anything else, Morten was white. He seemed to link his confidence to his physicality—he liked to joke about his Viking blood, though his beer belly would have seemed out of place at a raid—but he seemed unaware of where, exactly, his limbs ended, of which day of the week his beard went from scruffy to scraggly to downright rough. Whereas sometimes, when Pierre entered a room, Sita could swear Tchaikovsky's Peter motif was playing somewhere, jolly, in the background, Morten's perennial smile held no mischief, just blithe assurance. It rankled Sita that he thought he inspired anything in her but dread and a coincidental curiosity.

She'd mistaken Pierre for white until she'd suggested a Vietnamese place for dinner one night, and even then, only after she'd taken courage by his foreigner-status to divulge that she'd never tried it before, that though she'd moved to the city after college she'd only recently felt secure enough in her health insurance, her 401K, her no-longer-fake ID, to go out for a dinner she wasn't sure she'd like with the anticipation of paying for drinks afterwards. "I'll pay if you like it," Pierre had said, "and if you don't, Maman wouldn't stand for us to be together anyways." He'd been joking, maybe; they'd never made it to France to see Hang before it was too late to take stock in her opinion.

Morten's parents, meanwhile, owned the fishmonger, and in that first week, they saw them whenever Morten was hungry. "It won't turn you into a fish, Stella, I promise," he told her, after she'd turned down his parents' offer of a free fishcake for the third time and they began glaring at her before they even opened the door. "And poor Lars. He used to love them." He wasn't a complete imbecile. "I mean ... he seemed excited. To try them. After you and Pierre talk it over." She stumbled a bit as she fled, and of course it took him no time to catch up with her, and he wheeled Signe's tank in front of her, blocking her path. "Look, my mother could take her for the afternoon if you want to go out to the cabin."

When they arrived he wouldn't leave her alone. These are his woods, she tried to tell herself, but the words hung disparately in her mind; she couldn't find meaning in it, that the fruit she needed belonged to this tree-sized, fish-fed oaf. They lingered on the beach until she spotted a crab, and while Lars was entranced she mumbled something about the bathroom.

In the gloaming she wanted to linger. Two fruits—still only two, and still perfectly ripe—hung just above her eyes, where she could reach them on her toes. They must be accustomed to this place. Or did each rose apple have to learn anew that despite the chill on their skin, this sharp needled corner was all they would ever get? She needed to hurry, she reminded herself, but instead she plucked slowly, gently, and held a rose apple in each palm, and warmed them there. She would save one, she decided, not just for Lars but for him to share with Pierre. Once Pierre tasted its flesh he would remember and eschew all other.

"Here you are." Morten's voice was quiet, and when she spun, she saw that he held Lars, asleep, in his arms, but now he bent low and placed the baby on a patch of moss between two stones. She tucked the fruits into her sling, took a step back so the tree held her upright as he approached. "You left your son with me."

"He's fine," she said, but her heart paused until he nodded.

Morten's arm lunged past her to take hold of the tree's trunk, and her fruit-lined stomach nearly touched his. "What do you do when you're out here by yourself, Stella? Do you think of what might have been?"

She blinked. His face was all she could see now, for his fiery beard filled up her peripheral vision in both directions. "Yes."

"If this land had been yours?"

"Yes."

"I know American girls," he said. "I've known American girls."

"Yes," she said, and she wanted to close her eyes and get it over with, but if she lowered her eyelashes, they would brush his chin, and perhaps then Pierre would not believe her, afterwards.

Morten laughed, and she felt a rose apple fall from her as her jostled midsection resought its equilibrium. He took a step back and picked it up and bit into it, and grimaced. Throwing it behind him, he said, "You're not an American girl. Come on. Let's get the kid back before your husband gets home."

*

She had lain flat on the living room floor and forced Lars to crawl atop her to suckle so that when Pierre opened the door, and hung his suit, and looked for Lars, the baby looked like a conquering wolf. She opened her eyes and sat up as he pulled Lars off of her.

"Morton has to go out to the islands," he said. "Mona wants to see if she can concentrate on the competition with the baby nearby."

She pulled her neckline up.

"He also said he wouldn't go, except that you seemed fine." Pierre paused to kiss Lars on the nose, on the forehead, on each tiny ear. "Are you fine?"

"I got you a rose apple," she said, pulling it out of her pocket. Lars paused his squealing to reach for it, and for a moment their hands fell on it together. Pierre had always had warm hands, and his son's were even better. In the mild evening sunlight they sat together on the floor and considered the fruit.

"He'll be in daycare soon," Pierre said.

She didn't pretend to protest about how early it was, though she knew that his mother thought so. "Do you remember these from when you were little?"

Beside Lars, the fruit looked small and lovely and perfect. Beside Pierre, Lars did too. "Better than what I found," Pierre said, tilting his head back to his shopping bag, out of which were protruding carrots, a cabbage, and either a cucumber or a very sad squash, she couldn't tell. He held the fruit up to Lars' lips, and fixed his own around it, and Sita brought her face close to ready her teeth for a bite and marveled at how lovely the planes of his face were, this man who'd wrecked her. She prayed that this rose apple, far from the tree, was the best one yet.

"An owl," mouthed Mona, nodding her head to the west. They watched it silently, and Sita watched her dip a steel cup into the pale green water of the lake where it folded itself to rush down the falls. She pulled another out of her pack and dipped it full, too, before offering one to Sita. "Before you came there was a company that made lunchboxes shaped like owls. Can't even find them at the charity shop now."

Sita held it, let its weight settle in her palms, though she had no intention of drinking from a lake so open to other cups, other lips. Maybe next year. She had a full set of engraved steel dishware waiting for her in a box in her parents' basement whenever she wanted it; their wedding present to her, one they'd finally made the summer she'd turned fifteen and announced that she was a feminist who'd never change her last name. (Fine, said her mother, who'd never had to consider the question.) They'd told her about the gift as they shifted the box from suitcase to cedar closet, from high to higher shelf as priorities required. Her mother had wanted to mail it ahead, so it reached the village when they did, but she'd balked at the shipping costs and decided Sita could carry it with her next time she visited her childhood home. One day she would take Lars there, and one day, maybe, it would be his.

"One day I'll crochet Signe a little swan," she offered, and Mona seemed mollified, tipped the rest of her water into her wide mouth, pulling her sunglasses atop her head to rub at her eyes. They'd begun their ascent directly after dropping off the babies— no, toddlers, though Lars especially seemed determined to spend as much of his life as possible lying down—and Sita would have to let Mona do the talking, explain the delay, if they were called back to retrieve a child demanding an untimely end to the separation. They'd only started daycare last week. Sita had been embarrassed to see Mona again at drop-off; there was no way to pretend they'd never met, not here. When she'd complemented Sita's summer sweater—dove grey, Indian cross stich knit—and asked for a lesson some time, or maybe another little hike?, Sita had said yes despite the hesitations the lonely summer had brought. Morten had never reappeared to take her to the woods, so she'd stayed home with Lars lest in town he demanded fish, and when he napped she opened her e-mail to find, once a day since she'd been on her own again, a freshly reiterated summons from Bhoo-mija.

They twisted their shoulders for one last look at the fjord. To-day's ship was coming in, leaving a sundrenched wake that seemed a mile long. If Lars died tomorrow, she'd have to scatter his ashes there; Lake Michigan meant nothing to him, nor the Ganges. No, Pierre would balk, and she would acquiesce. If only she were Vishnu, whose steps would cover all of it; she'd ended up more like Mahabali, hadn't she? Bhoomija's parents were the only ones she knew who celebrated Onam, and she'd loved the story, loved the gentleness and the wrath, the way it recognized that the first day of school was really when everything began.

It was late summer. The shells in the rock pools they'd left be-neath them took on a green cast; the ones on dry land were white and brittle, and, often, broken. It wasn't Labor Day here, the land where owls flew in daylight. But years ago—at the end of that feminist summer, before the Onasadya feast—they'd unfurled themselves onto a chhattai in her backyard, topped their shik-hanjis up with far too much vodka, and taken a vow to live hon-estly, without shame or subterfuge, New Brown Girls, capital-ized, and one of them, after all, in a spangled red and black bikini she'd told Bhoomija she'd wear in public, later. Sita had failed in small ways and large. At pool parties she would leave her shirt on until the second before her body hit the water, whipping it off her head with her knees already shaking with the shock of the cold.

"I will never pretend to care about football," Sita'd called out into the level suburban wind, imagining a chasm much like this mountain, this fjord, for her words to swoop and soar in.

"I will never pretend to care about anything other than brown girls," Bhoomija had cried.

That seems limiting, she'd wanted to say, but the words would have put an end to the moment, she knew it, so instead she said, "Way to go full lesbo-erotic." She'd been awful.

"Yeah, yeah," said Bhoomija, and though Sita had tried to bring up the vow from time to time after graduation, Bhoomija pretended that, like so many things, it had all been just a trick of the light. But she couldn't have forgotten. Micah had emailed her when she was pregnant to tell her he'd moved in with her in New York, but he was worried. Things had really begun to unravel, he wrote. It wasn't money, somehow she had enough money, but she jumped when the phone rang, winced when he suggested a night in. She'd written back that she'd never known Bhoomija to sit through an entire movie, that's why Bollywood films had songs, and who didn't jump when the phone rang?

"Do you think they are okay?" Mona asked.

The owls? Sita considered, then recalibrated. "You saw how excited Signe was to be around those big kids," she said.

"Still," said Mona. "This is the beginning of everything for them, isn't it? It took two weeks for the other tots to start telling me and Tawfiq Salah we smelled of poo."

Sita looked at her. "What did you do?"

Mona raised her eyebrow. "What do you do? We couldn't not go. And then I learned how to surf, and it didn't matter, that kind of thing."

Sita narrowed her eyes to the water, tried to see it from Mona's eyes, as someplace she could go, someplace she could do battle instead of a vast bulwark against the past. From nearby it looked greener but now, from where they stood, it was strong and blue, lapis lazuli, and every crash against the fjord meant a wave, out there, on the islands, too strong and vicious. Sita wanted to weave a net around each crest, and Mona, to stand upon it. Well, perhaps it was a small bulwark against the past, for Mona.

"I've always wanted to learn to knit," Mona said, and Sita realized she'd not responded. "Every Norwegian can do it."

"You can't, ergo not every Norwegian," Sita said.

Mona laughed. "Would you teach me?"

"Right now?" Sita had a few balls of yarn in her rucksack, but she was at work on the woolen pants she'd been told Lars wouldn't survive a week in daycare without: a thin merino, maroon and slippery.

"No, next week. Tuesday. Wednesday. Any morning after I

help at the mosque, before I'm off for practice, or any Saturday after a meet. We could meet at the pier for a bit until it gets too cold. You could teach me how to make mittens for my mum's birthday; she can't knit either, even after all this time." She looked down at Sita and frowned. "Sita. Come on. You can't make me ask Morten's sister."

"Okay," Sita said, though what she wanted to say was that this was the first time anyone had ever asked her. That she'd love to. That the thought made the day's cool warmth feel molten in her chest, like a proper summer's heat. That even though the summer was ending she'd lived it.

*

Sita had walked around the mountain many times, and halfway up dozens to rest at various lakes, but Mona had promised that the view from the top—the convergence of all the views at once—was worth the climb. She'd wanted to celebrate with Sita, here, before telling everyone else about the baby-to-come. It would be an Easter baby, born into a village more calm than usual while the inhabitants were away in their cabins, but Sita promised to be in town, as though she'd ever go anywhere else. Pierre had made noises about buying a car, a boat, a cabin, but Hang had never found work again after that spring, so half his paycheck was mailed to a flat in Paris Sita might never see. And Sita had no qualms about admitting that the mountain itself grew more lovely the higher they climbed: moss and grass fell away, and the purple saxifrage clung to grey stone and cast delicate shadows on the reflected oranges and pinks of the sunrise at their back. They had climbed high enough that ice was no longer intermittent, and the walking stick Mona had lent her no longer seemed an object of laughter. If they didn't tarry at the top they would join the sun for a shared descent and watch its reflection: a glaze on the open sea.

"Signe's beyond excited about the Halloween outfit," Mona said. Sita had garbled together a wool and chiffon and bead concoction for—what else?—a princess costume, a green and pink lengha that would stand out in a crowd of Annas and Elsas. Lars was wearing his normal clothes, woolen things that kept him warm and dry and reasonably clean. "It's sweet, isn't it? Their little romance?"

"They're children, Mona."

With no regards for her misgivings Lars had become the most popular toddler at daycare: his teachers were somehow convinced, and had convinced his classmates, that black hair signified royal blood, that he was a prince from a faraway land, sent to rule. Sita tried to remind him that his grandmother Hang was by no means a queen, but Pierre was tickled, and while they folded the interminable laundry he would stage whisper to his son that Sita didn't know, but Mémère's grand-maman had ruled all of Indochina, and when he was big, they would sail there in a boat and reclaim their castle. How Signe had become involved Sita did not know, but she assumed it involved Pierre and Morten's toddler Saturdays at the cabin while she walked with Mona to her surf competitions on the outer islands, or to else just down to the fjord, where they sat on the shore with bottles of water and bagfuls of fraying skeins and if Mona's yarn felt uncooperative she sighed and dove off the pier, wrestled the frigid waves, and won.

Sita slipped, just about, on the ice that, by next week, would make its way into the village, and then found her footing, and saw that Mona had reached the summit and was waiting. She'd forgotten to turn the lights off on her reflective wristband, and so the red dots alternated with a reversed stripe of the painted sky. Sita wasn't alone here. Not on this continent, not in the country, not even on this mountain. Why couldn't she convince her heart that this was true?

She planted herself beside Mona and exhaled. The sun had followed them up, and all around them, the village and the woods unrolled into the sea. To the east she could see the road to the cabin, and wished she could ask Mona what Morten was like with her family, if it mattered. Instead she said, "I've been thinking about matching Christmas sweaters for Pierre, Lars, and his mother. Is red and green cable knit too obvious, or just classic?"

"They'll go again this year?" Mona asked.

Sita nodded.

"And you'll stay with us?"

They descended the mountain at its back, racing against the sun to minimize their time in the woods in the dark. But Sita had no sense of where the path would veer, and the coming child tested Mona's balance, and soon Sita found herself staring into the stars. "Mona?" she said. "Are you all right?"

"I'm just waiting—look," she whispered. Mona'd crouched down on the path, her back against stone rather than at the mercy of the wind, and in front of her the lights danced with abandon. "Signe and Lars must be thrilled." Sita crouched down next to Mona, unsure of where to look, eventually setting on the bridge of Mona's nose. Mona didn't return her half-gaze as she continued, "But up here, Sita, it's just you and me. It's rare I get time with someone who doesn't see me as just the fishmonger, or just another refugee's kid, or just another girl in the family, or no, not just another one: the rebellious one, the one who married out. And I value it. But maybe I've been pushing myself onto you?"

As Mona spoke, there was nothing else: Sita stared at the lights and she didn't know who made the ads; they didn't flicker. They came and they stayed and then there was nothing you could do but think about them, and about how lucky you were to be alive. "No, it's just—" But if she could have mentioned Morten, she already would have. She forced her head to turn and look at Mona. "I hate Christmas."

Mona's laugh, and her own, mingled in the afternoon darkness, and Sita had forgotten what it was to laugh; she'd forgotten what it was to stare into the eyes of someone who felt—even as you knew it wasn't true, even as you liked that it wasn't true— just like you. "Morten would have expected you to knit sweaters for all of us," Mona said. "He keeps asking me to knit him one in Glimt colors. Jesus, man, let me knit a proper scarf before I attempt to swathe your gut!"

"I am actually knitting you and Signe sweaters," Sita admitted. She unfurled her scarf and swung it round her again, twice. "I could knit Morten one, too, if you want? It's too late for Glimt bumblebees, though—yours are green and gold."

Mona smiled at her. "I'd love that."

Sita slipped, and Mona caught her wrist, but the ground was almost flat now. They were at a bus shelter; if they waited seventeen hours, they could flag the next bus around the mountain, back into the village and then, via ferry, through the fjord and beyond. But no, she could see Mona texting; soon their ride would appear, and they'd be home. This year, she hadn't bothered to remind Pierre about Navami: nothing new fit her, and her kajal was just a nub unfit even for giving Lars a kaala tika to go with the buff—transverse herringbone stitch in sky blue, her mother's

favorite color—she'd finished last night instead of singing to Cha-
mundi. She hadn't done anything: but maybe she could cook. If
there was nothing to be had in this country but milk she could
make barfi and regale Lars with exploits of the goddess. She could
paint him a picture.

Sita left the mosque's first winter charity festival after filling two
boxes with washed sheets and cans of soup and gently used house
slippers, and Mona, curled in upon herself, didn't insist. Before
she answered any of the emails that had lined up in the box—the
sender column reading Bhoomija Bhoomija Bhoomija Bhoomija
Bhoomija times a hundred—Sita made her first Norwegian phone
call. She knew his number because his website outlined his office
hours on Tuesdays and Thursdays, via e-mail if they simply
clicked, or via phone if they called his office number, so long as
he was in his office. Often, his website said, he was out on field-
work in the city, pursuing his research on Midwestern Latin food
truck culture. Sita wasn't sure, anymore, if food trucks were open
on Christmas Eve, or if they had once been open and had since,
like everything else, wrestled their way back in fits and starts.
Still, he wasn't in his office. She let the phone's light dim and re-

alized she hadn't yet drawn the kitchen curtains. Parso, when Pierre and Lars had left, had been the day before the new moon, and when she looked at the sky now it seemed as though no time had passed.

She'd forgotten to go to the store and now the fridge was full of cooked food in tupperwares, labelled in Pierre's sharp cursive, doomed to rot, but no onions, no ginger, no garlic, nothing he might have left her to chop. She could barely remember the real taste of cilantro. There was wine in the fridge, and half a pot of heavy cream, and cinnamon sticks in a jar next to the stovetop. She wondered if they would write, when wet, and ran one under the sink, hot water promising her everything would be okay if she would just give herself up to it—she shook her head—and tried to write on the window. Devanagri script, backwards, so if the world were different, someone might read her name from the outside.

Her breasts had stopped leaking. When she saw her shirt's reflection it wasn't obvious—the milk stains from yesterday were still half-moons, one slashed by the t-shirt pocket—but her nipples were hard against the dried stains and she wondered if this might be the end. If it was there was nothing stopping her from doing as Bhoomija was asking. She needed Sita.

She left the paisley scarf on its hook by the door; properly wrapped, she wouldn't be able to hear well enough. There were lights on the road: not only the strings hung from the trees, but headlights turning out of the parking lot beside the stave church, each pair leaving the village in their own way. They clouded over the sky and she was grateful, and steadied, and when she got to the top of the hill she looked out over the islands she could not see, and did not wait, but dialed.

After she identified herself there was a pause, and in that pause Sita thought: yes. I have to go, yes—and soon, for if he has forgotten me I will throw myself into the sea. "Sita!" he said, and she hadn't heard her name pronounced quite this way for a long time and she jumped and missed the landing, and as she fell to her knees she cried out and then his tone took on a deep, easy warmth. "Are you okay?"

I am as tall as Lars, now, she realized. The islands appeared at eye level, level too with the moon, which she'd told Nenn had been made of cheese and had then neglected to tell her son. The anthropology of food, she thought. Keep talking, she wanted to say.

He did, sidestepping his previous question with the ease she knew he hadn't lost. "Are you still clicking and clacking away?" A pause, then: "Knitting, I mean. I hope not typing up memos for insurance; Micah said you'd fallen in love with a Frenchman and left us." And last: "Though I shouldn't speak ill of insurance, the years we've had."

This was all she would get, she knew, unless she came up with something. "He's lovely, the Frenchman. Pierre." Mona had brought up, lightly, the idea of returning to insurance, and then, in response to her doubts, given her a real offer of employment at the fishmonger—part-time, in case that was what worried her, getting the washing done and the shopping in; Mona'd learned it quickly and she would, too, and when she wasn't tutoring the new arrivals or at her proper job, out on the waves, they'd share the work, it would be fun—and Sita had repeated Pierre's suggestion, that she wait until their second was in daycare, too, neutrally, without adding her own thoughts on the matter, and now she wished she had done anything so that she had something more to say. "How's the book?" she asked, because there must be one, in some state.

"Oh, you're wonderful to ask. Everyone else is too afraid to. Though," his voice dropping to whisper, albeit not a real one, "they're right to be. I'm absolutely stalled." She pictured him winking. He'd begun to pace, his footsteps on the linoleum coming through clearly, in neat rhythm. In his normal voice he went on, "Well, it's been wonderful to hear from you," and she realized she'd sat picturing for too long. She rose and stretched, leaning forward on the balls of her feet—the stance of the third beat in the song, where on the fifth, she'd spin onto the stage, opposite Bhoomija, lenghas wide like Madhuri's in Anjaam.

"I've had a baby," she said, and heard his footsteps falter.

"Well, Sita, that's fantastic! I'm so glad I got to hear the news! Is the little one healthy? Are you doing all right?"

Had she told Micah about Lars? Or Bhoomija? She wasn't sure. After the first year she'd slowed the pace of her responses as they had, to let them lose interest without guilt. Nothing in Bhoomija's latest message, with links to the testing requirements and the airlines webpages, indicated that she understood that Sita was changed. Still, it seemed impossible that Bhoomija could be unaware.

"Sita? Are you doing all right?"

She imagined asking him if she should go to New York, if she should move to New York. She cradled the phone in her lap and let him call her name until she was sure she had transmuted all her milk into tears, and her tears, now, into rivulets of ice down her neck, and pushed to put an end to the call, and pushed to rise up onto her feet and start her descent home.

*

Though she'd called Mona from the bottom of the hill, it was Morten who brought the car around. She slipped into the passenger's seat and remembered she'd forgotten their sweaters, a bottle of wine, her toothbrush, only when they were past the village, past the fjord and on their way on the empty road inland.

She remembered her shirt and kept her coat on, and maybe it was this, she decided to tell herself, that led Morten to park, and close the ignition, and, in the darkness, remark, "I suppose, Stella, you'll want a walk around the trees before you come inside."

She nodded, and though she wasn't sure she could be seen, as she stepped gingerly into the trees she felt him behind her. If she wanted to lose her tail she had to know where she was going; until she found herself at the little lakeshore she wasn't sure she'd been anywhere near, and now she exhaled, and looked over the ice for a minute before turning back. She could gauge, she thought, how far she'd overstepped.

"Do you skate?" he asked. She couldn't look directly at him; though he had just one reflector on, a small one on his ankle, as though he were being monitored, it was by far the brightest light in the woods. She nodded as she blinked. "Okay, then," he said. From the crevasse at the foot of the tree nearest his ankle, where, when Sita looked, she pictured gnomes, he pulled out a thermos bag and, from within, two pairs of skates. "You'll be unsteady in Mona's," he said, "but they'll have to do."

He crouched down in front of her and took her foot, slid it from its boot and into the bladed one between his legs. Then the other. She had stopped breathing, she realized, and when he let go to pull his own boots up over his prodigious calves she gasped to refill her chest. He bent his elbow and held it out to her as though they were at a nineteenth-century picnic. There is nothing to understand, she tried telling herself, even as she tried to step backwards, then on reconsideration forwards towards the water. He wants to skate. Her steps achieved nothing. Was she supposed to slice through the snow for these few inches, until the ice began? She listened for his footsteps while turned away, but it was quiet. There were no cicadas here.

"I'm going to pick you up," he said, from behind her; she could see the reflection of his legs in the silvery white ground. When his hands touched her waist she lurched forward, and he tightened his hold. For a second she was removed: her feet could feel nothing below, and when she looked up, the stars beckoned, the ornis promising, maybe, to keep their distance. She remembered the view from the airplane window as a child, the Caspian Sea so far below the stars by the wings that it felt farther than space. She remembered the day their ferry turned the corner into the fjord; she'd worn white, marital and mournful, and adjusted her red bangles with her reddened fingertips and hope had made her feel she might soar the last mile, carried on the wind. Morten had been here on each occasion. As his name passed through her mind his clawy hands left her, her feet deposited on an unyielding surface. She brought her hands forward to protect her face as she fell but instead his arm was around her stomach, pushing it in, pulling her up. "You said you knew how. So do it."

By the time her toes scratched a hold in the ice he'd skated away, his red light twinkling in the distance like a yuletide star. The ice must be safe, she understood, and though she had been telling the truth, skating on the lake was nothing like at Millennium Park. Instead of feeling her legs move to the beat of radio carols, she found them keeping pace with her own heart, faster and faster. She raised her hands about her head and though she could not twirl she let her left leg glide in a circle and the icy remnants of tears on her neck slide down past her breasts onto her stomach, and when she blinked nothing changed: darkness, and then darkness, and then darkness. She was back at the start, at the first death, the beginning of everything her soul had seen. She could never leave here. Oh, Bhoomija, she whispered, how could you ask me to go?

PART THREE

There would be no springtime by Easter. Still, Mona and Sita sat at the pub window, willing the snow to stop swirling over the fjord long enough to let the sunrise through, or the sunset: they had all day. Mona was determined to finish matching blankets for Signe and Ronja before Ronja's birth—purled ladders in a cheerful, chunky lilac; she felt too pregnant to surf, too pregnant even to stand near the fish at her would-be in-laws' shop, and so, she'd told Sita, she hoped for more daytime company, positively needed it. The advice against getting together in private homes had long since been lifted but Mona preferred the pub. That way, she laughed, I don't have to pick up the floor. They'd met at five past noon so they could nurse their beers until it was time to pick up the children.

Sita hoped the green walls and cracked leather booths would have a calming effect on her; here, like nowhere else in the village, she could be anywhere. But if she could imagine herself at a dodgy bar in the city, then, maybe, she shouldn't be in this one. The professor had e-mailed today, asking for her phone number, reiterating his congratulations, but wondering—just making sure—if he hadn't heard tears? He was glad things were working out with Pierre. He was attaching an article Micah had sent him about Quechua women who faced shocks in early motherhood, how it correlated with negative outcomes for their children, rather than the most recent draft article he was writing, about the pandemic and food trucks. Would she call him back, please? He'd left a personal number. Correlation, not causation, she muttered. Instead of responding she'd clicked open each message from Bhoomija until the box was empty.

"Sita?"

She turned back to Mona, to the bright blue and bright red and clean white lines, the flag for her children to lie underneath when things got chilly. She'd dropped a stitch, and Sita took the needles from her hands to fix it, and saw that she'd dropped another stitch earlier in the line and began to undo the shoddy work and then thought better of it and looked up. "Do you want me to do this?" She'd taken to that language with Lars, who ignored her unless he was distraught and then muzzled against her until she invited him to nurse. He had become interested in flowers now; Hang had taught him how they grew, why they differed, what messages they might convey. In the afternoons he walked her from the daycare to Pierre's office slowly, thoughtfully, telling her where he expected each bloom come summer. Pierre would bring him carnations from the supermarket and he would rip them to bits and then caress each fallen petal lovingly.

Mona was talking, she realized, and she handed back the work in time for to hear complaints against her sister-in-law's new partner, who asked her if she'd be knitting the children blankets from her own country, as well, as though this wasn't it, as though—while Mona described his tiny smirk and his undoubtably tinier penis, Sita caught sight of Morten and Pierre walking back from the pier; they must have left the office for hot dogs. She'd been so sure that day, on the lake; she'd fallen into a feverish sleep when she'd finally arrived at the cabin, had risen only to see Morten beside her head like an angry ghost, spooning bland carrot soup into her mouth. She wasn't contagious, she'd wanted to explain; Mona could be here instead. After the holiday they kept her at their house in the village until Pierre returned; the steady drone of the television had sharpened her language skills, perhaps, and driven her to hold fast to the night, to bring it forward when she could. And it was easy, now, in the dying and incomplete darkness of the village. She felt skinless as a jellyfish, though fleshy as ever, no matter Lars' dwindling dependence.

She might take that job, chopping the heads off the fish, doling out Arctic gefilte to light-eyed children, and give Pierre the money to buy the cabin he'd had his eye on. But it wasn't on the same lake, and it didn't have the same trolls nearby, the same monstrously large hands keeping her from utter disaster, from New York and everything her departure might mean. Bhoomija would have taken that tiny-dicked man and drawn his member next to a shivlingam, crossed them both out and made that the cover of her magazine. No, the back cover, inside; the cover would feature a woman. She'd have stayed up all night, would stay up all night until April, to have it online by spring.

*

She'd left after her second beer, her head unable to bear another second of Scandi-fisherman-nostalgia-pop, and Mona hadn't insisted. She'd found a branch near the stave church and fashioned a walking stick from it and pulled herself up the hill and considered what she might write to the professor; as the offices emptied she thought back to if Mona had offered to pick up Lars from daycare and thought she probably had. Pierre's office light was on. She didn't know which window was Morten's but saw him emerge, then, from the back door. He was walking towards her, after a fashion, in that he was not walking straight into the fjord; he was not the type to give himself up to the sea. He had a bulbous bag hung from his shoulder and she realized he'd not been scared off from, or wised up to the dangers to, communal exercise. The gym sat in the beautiful stone clinic building that also housed a florist, a key cutter, and the municipal snow-clearing offices. She decided to go down to buy Lars flowers; they had a wider selection than simple carnations. Though she knew they weren't in season she thought they might have roses, red, whetting the villagers' romantic desires, their wintery fears; Lars would enjoy using the thorns to pierce holes in the petals like she did with mattri dough.

She'd fallen, and as she disposed of the stick she brushed her coat free of ice and used her scarf to dry her face. Morten had been listening to something as he turned the corner to the gym; the small white pods in his ears were some way, she thought, of ensuring he never had time to think. Never had time to worry. She stared in the window and watched him impassively scan his phone over the entry portal, watched him peel his warmer layers off and hang them from a coat rail right there in public—how safe it was, here—and peel his office layers off to reveal bright orange shorts and a matching top, like a builder unafraid for his extremities. He would tell her to go, if she explained the situation. Even if she didn't, he would tell her to go, to leave his wife and his town well enough alone and go sparkle like a snowflake across the sea. He would smile as he said it; he wouldn't specify which sea lay between here and her home, the imminence of the water plausible deniability he didn't need or care for.

There were hands on her shoulders, lips on her lips, and when she wrested herself free she found Pierre, looking wounded. "Mona said she'd keep Lars for dinner," he said, "so I thought I'd surprise you with flowers instead."

For a minute, the clouds parted; she turned, with Pierre, to the west, and the sky was orange and purple and blue and grotesquely beautiful. "So you did," she said.

In a minute his face was rearranged, and his impish smile in its place of honor on his chiseled face. "So did you, it seems. We're ridiculous. Should we skip the flowers and go have sex?"

In bed he kissed her again, undenied. "Happy anniversary," he said.

"It isn't," she said.

"It was last week," he agreed, "but we're here, now. And it's been almost three years since we arrived," he added, his hands snaking down her throat, raking across her nipples. "If you claim your citizenship soon we can all go together to France for Easter without having to wait in any lines."

"There are tests," she said, covering her gut with the blanket.

"Okay, Christmas," he said, easily. He uncovered her, trailed kisses down to her belly button, looked up. "Joyeux anniversaire, ma femme nue."

When Pierre left to go fetch Lars she clicked on her e-mail, read Bhoomija's messages again, swallowed, and hit delete.

Pierre had made a fouace loaf; they walked to the clinic with Lars and explained that Signe was now a sister. There was no one on the streets; it was cold and humid, and Sita thought of how it had all come together this year: Easter and Holi, even Ramadan, though Mona was of course in no place to fast. Whatever it was—Emerson's big ocean, perhaps, which Sita claimed as her own for lack of a more domesticated term—it was clear that this spring was one for renewal.

Ronja—Morten had sung a song to go with her name, and Lars seemed to know it—was curled up on her mother's breast, and Sita felt her own chest stop, and assess, and deflate, and she felt her breaths quicken, but Pierre's hand was at her back, leading her in, cooing at the new arrival. Morten took the bread and broke off a piece with his hands and held it up to Mona's lips and Sita wondered if he was happy.

Pierre took the baby into his arms and bent his knees, just a little, so Lars could see without poking his fingers near, so he could stare at the baby, as he was doing now, with a look so tender and familiar Sita wanted to heave. She held up a hand—wait—and backstepped out of the room, the ward, the building, the only beautiful one in the village, the only one made of stone and built to last, because people would always be sick, and though they would be born sometimes more often, lately, they would die. It had begun to rain, not forcefully, and Sita breathed in droplets along with air. Her chest was trying to pound away at her brain, convince her to match Mona baby for baby, with an urgency even Pierre seemed to have lost. Her feet were ready to leave. She wondered if there was anywhere to get a drink at the clinic. Nowhere in town right now, not for days.

She could leave. By the end of the week she'd be in New York, where she knew no one who cared about Easter or Holi or Ramadan or babies. She could get a drink that necessitated the flashing of her expired driver's license, where her hair was brushed. Micah would buzz her into the building where she would let Bhoomija make a comment about how fat she'd gotten and how dumb she was to leave a husband Bhoomija hadn't thought much of in the first place—and the child—and Sita would gauge whether or not that could be followed up by a comment about how giving birth was at least better than creating something and throwing it all away on some sort of wavery, unmoored principle, or whether she would be gracious, compliment the way Bhoomi-ja'd repurposed furniture she'd found on the street, added jeweled-toned paint and made it fusion as though Sita and Draupadi and Shakuntala had never seen a floral pastel.

When she returned to the room, Morten and Pierre were leading the children out with promises of bubbles and fishcakes and sightings of the American servicemen in their funny outfits. Mona was staring down at the baby, and Sita nestled herself into the bedside chair before they each looked up. Oh, but the baby's eyes were a deep, coal black. Mona's were tired, and Sita handed her the ice water from the little table. "When's your family coming round?" she asked.

"They came this morning, but they'll be back," Mona said, and groaned. "You all right?"

Sita blushed. "I'd forgotten."

"Me, too," said Mona. "Or else I wouldn't be here again. God. But good thing, eh, little one?" Sita watched them speak, watched a bond stretch and strengthen and shine until it felt intrusive, and then stood up to go. "Come by the house tomorrow, okay?"

Sita nodded.

The first boat out wasn't until the day after.

*

They'd learned to knit on Holi in the second grade, when they'd been tasked with making blankets for a city shelter the school had partnered with. Bhoomija, left-handed, had given up immediately and taken out her diary to capture the idiocy of it all in verse. It was a stupid thing to be good at, maybe: was it an art? (They were in history class, about to start—as per their teacher's bubbly intro—a unit on women's history that would last the rest of the year! Herstory!) So: men didn't knit. The pictures on the projector showed white women and girls in black and white, creating, and the pictures of the shelter on the wall showed Black woman and children, receiving. There was no one Black in Sita's class. Maricela and Joshua were Mexican. Amy was Filipina, but spoke Spanish. Bhoomija couldn't wait until they started Spanish in fourth grade so they could understand more of what was being said at their five-person lunch table. By the time they graduated she was fluent.

Sita would never be fluent in Spanish but knitting: that she could do. The sheer painstaking slowness of the endeavor awed her, hushed her, captured her, she knew even then, for life. She could barely hear Bhoomija, mouthy, in response to a suggestion that they should be on the receiving end of the blankets. That knitting was history, and they weren't even in America when it had happened. No one ever expected her to speak up, thankfully, but now they didn't even expect her to listen: she was busy.

Sita took to bringing her needles everywhere, and that in-
cluded kitty parties where they were given a tray of pea-less sa-
mosas and ketchup and left to fend for themselves in the basement or the backyard, whichever the parents weren't using.
Bhoomija had always brought her notebook, and Sita had always
sat with her, lumpen, and now she felt less so. They were in the
basement that year—an early Holi, a late snowfall—and the host's
mother had come and sit beside her. She namaste-d, aap kaise ho-
ed rhetorically, but this time: an answer. Kamla would have been
so thrilled. Kaun? Your nani. I forget we don't have names, to you.
Of course we met: they came to visit in, what, '92? We all piled in
the station wagon and went to Niagara Falls. By the time we came
back she'd knit the most beautiful blanket I'd ever seen—thin as
a Kashmiri shawl. Of course you don't know: they used to pull
them through an anghooti to prove they were real. Well, I suppose
your parents must have it somewhere. Such a sweet girl. How are
you doing at school these days?

At home she'd pulled through the old suitcases, her mother bemused, unhelpful. She couldn't remember her knitting, though
of course she'd loved to weave when she was little—my nanaji was
a cloth merchant, Sita, you knew that! We took you past his shop
in—wait, no, she did know what had happened to it, she announced, then, aggravatingly, took a slow sip of her chai. They'd
taken the blanket to India with them: well, more for the plane

than for the country, they needed something to wrap her up in in the bassinet. Then her nani had taken it apart and used the yarn for something else.

When Sita had asked her mother to teach her how to weave, her mother had laughed, explained how she'd barely held her hand up to a needle since she'd shown an aptitude for numbers, a desire to study. They went to the mall that weekend and got a play loom, and soon Sita was helping herself to her parents' graph paper to try and figure out, if she could, how her mother's saris were put together. They always looked idiotic re-presented in cheap yarn, and she couldn't bring herself to ask her mother if she could pull one apart to seize its silk threads. Knitting into mittens or scarves, they looked different. Intentional, which they were. Bright, which she wanted to be. Warm, which she feared she was not. Lars, conversely, had been created so quickly.

When she'd finished the red paisley scarf, she'd been planning to drive up with Bhoomija to a classmates' graduation party at his lake house, but it was late, and her eyes hurt, and she was already tired of seeing these people she'd never think of again. "I'm sorry," she'd told Bhoomija over the phone. "I got caught up."

Bhoomija hadn't been calmed. "Well, you could have called before you got caught up."

She'd sat shivering at the party, nursing a bottle of hard lemonade. Without anything else to do with her hands the drink went down faster. A white boy who'd made fun of her hairy legs in junior high now sat down beside her on the porch stairs and put his hand on her shaved thigh, below the hem of her denim skirt. "Great night, isn't it?" he said.

His hand was cold, his eyes blurry, some kind of watery color. Still, she'd known him for the entire time she'd been thinking about the scarf, she realized. Longer. He'd been there that day, too, though she had no memory of his cold fingers tucked around the needles. "I finally did it," she told him.

He didn't ask what; it didn't come up. When she woke up the next morning she found herself in Bhoomija's guestroom. Bhoomija was sitting in front of the vanity, her ironed hair loose over her back in the mirror. When Sita blinked she smirked and turned her drawing around: Sita as Aurora, sleeping princess, spindle on the nightstand. When Sita got home her scarf was still lying flat on the bedspread, worsted weight so hardly thin, but delicate-looking, uncanny: paisleys in wool, red and intricate as a bride's mehndi. She wound the scarf around her neck. For once, she thought: something of my own.

She left in the morning, while everyone else was at the parade. Mona had sent her a thank you selfie for the embroidered green hijab; Sita was out of practice, and at several points had been unable to find her needle's way out through the thick wool—the trick was that you had to be prepared to abandon the grain of the weave—but it looked okay, serviceable. Lars was wearing one of the cheap boys' versions that had been clogging the shops since Easter—Pierre had come home with it one day, and Lars had taken it as his due. It was warm, sunny, exactly the day everyone wanted for the 17th, and after she reached the first lake and dipped her flask into the water, she unwrapped her paisleys from her neck and shoved them into her coat pocket unsuccessfully.

By the time she reached the top she could see the earliest climbers starting their ascent; she'd pass them on the way down, she had never become quite fast enough. She looked the other way, instead, faced inland, where it was just mountains and lingering patches of ice, trees with leaves hesitant to appear, dandelions almost ready to bloom. She'd never reached the summit, if you could call it that, without Mona. But she was here to speak nonetheless.

She dialed. It was past midnight there, but what did that matter? He'd been woken up by the hospital paging his wife often enough. Still, she was surprised to find his voice as smooth as ever, assuming she was Micah, asking if he needed help.

"It's Sita, actually."

"Sita! How's the baby?"

She closed her eyes, though the air wasn't the same, was it? Before long it would smell of cheap grilled meat and spilled beer, but for now it smelled of nothing. It was summer, almost, but still cold enough that the plants gave off nothing. Still. Nothing was something. And his voice, as always, its downward cadence and familiar accent. "He's so different from me," she began. He's always laughing at me, she remembered, so she added a laugh into what she went on with. "Well, that's always true, isn't it?" The air was unadulterated, but her head hurt. She fell silent.

"And how are you?"

"I'm," she began, so he wouldn't hang up. She felt her haseena morphing into tears and forced it down her throat. "I'm overlooking a fjord," she explained.

A pause. "Well, you know what Eriksen says about fjords," the professor said, though he carried on as if, rightly, she did not. She remembered reading Eriksen for her Metlife paper, which meant he'd written about desis. "*If you're Norwegian, you know them, but that doesn't mean you position yourself in relation to them the same way as your countrymen.*"

"Compatriots," Sita said.

"That's my girl," said the professor, and then he stopped and swallowed, and she felt her cheeks suck themselves in between her teeth so she could bite on them.

She knew she had just one more chance to keep him on the line. When she tasted blood, the memory returned and she argued, "Eriksen shouldn't be taken seriously about fjords; he wrote about Mauritius. Bhajans in Creole. *Bhaji on the Beach.*" Which wasn't Eriksen at all—it had been her mother's favorite film—but she was getting somewhere now that he was listening. "Once, I'd thought of the water as an ending," she said.

"Sita?" he asked.

"Pierre didn't mind us spending weekends walking aimlessly. When we reached the lake, we'd walk north or south until we knew a beach was about to arrive, and buy picnic foods and unwrap the scarves from our faces to kiss, boldly, our presence muffled by the snow and the crashing waves. He insisted there was no such thing as the upper peninsula, that if we swam north we'd reach Atlantis, surely, but I told him there was no chance: it was water, like turtles, all the way down. It would just be us, at sea, forever." She closed her eyes, then opened them, turned so she could see the water, ignoring the well-preserved walkers in swishy pants. Morten had gotten Pierre a set for his birthday in a lurid chartreuse. "But we got here, and then he got me a pet, as if I needed something else to worry about."

"Sita," the professor said, more gently than she'd expected of an interruption, "do you find yourself worried a lot nowadays?"

This time her laugh wasn't to mirror; it just fell out of her, a dented bell. "What's there to worry about now?" But there was the foghorn; a ship coming in as she leaned away from it, as she spoke, bringing, she supposed, anything. "How's Micah finding New York?"

"Do you worry about the baby? Or about being alone with him?"

She straightened herself. How dare he not speak to her for years and then: this. Nenn had just been an animal. He hadn't had a heart. Well, he'd had a heart; it was something else cognitive animals lacked, the inability to prioritize artha over kama, or the other way around—purusharthas did not apply to beings for whom all existence could be nothing but the discharging of dharma. He wasn't a purush like Lars, with whom she was often, without disaster, alone.

"It's been far safer for children here than it has there," she said, though: in the utensils drawer sat the iodine tablets his teachers had given her for Lars to take should the Russians drop the bomb to take control of the shipping routes. She'd told Pierre to memorize their shape, and crushed the box between her fingertips until it was too flat to make any further sound.

"Still is," he agreed, and he did not sound contrite at all. She wondered if he approved of Bhoomija, and how much more ambitious she was when she destroyed things.

She opened her eyes, turned. The meager parade was snaking up the main road and she looked down upon them all. If she hurried down to the lake, she might have time for a swim before they swarmed.

When the others came in for a break before the cabin, she huddled further into the duvet, wishing she was dressed underneath it. Her swim had been bracing and her hair had dried into brushwidthed pieces; the water hadn't quenched her anger but transmuted it into something harder to articulate but more familiar. Ronja had been left outside the door in her stroller and Sita wished Signe had, too, for the girl was twirling in front of her, demanding admiration, and she had grown beyond the marshmallow stage; Sita wanted to give it to her, but what could she do beyond clapping, the trembling that had seized her body muffling each round of applause? The girl knew her light: she danced in the shaft coming in from between the curtains, blocking Sita into her corner, until Morten pulled them open. Lars had opened the fridge for him, was explaining what pears were, and apples, and how—when had he learned this?—the cheese had been made.

Pierre, of all people, came and sat down on the edge of the couch; he put his warm hand on her bare shoulder. Once, this would have been enough to stop the trembling. "I had to give your father your number," he said. "He had something he wanted to tell you directly, this afternoon."

On cue her phone rang. She looked at Pierre, handed it to him.

He shook his head, handed it back, closed her fingers around it so tightly she thought it might emerge a butterfly. "Take it in the bedroom," he suggested.

She dressed before she came back out; the others were pulling on their shoes and hats. Mona undid her buckles and came over with her bag. "I wanted to thank you for this!" she said, pointing at her own head.

"You did, with the picture," Sita replied.

"Yes, but also with this," Mona said, thrusting a pile of wool at her. As Sita took it and found its edges with her fingers she saw that it was a scarf, red selburoses on a white background, with white stars on each end, and blue diamond edging. It was more complicated than anything she'd seen Mona attempt before. "For Norway. And America. For you."

"Come on," said Pierre. "Wrap yourself in your new scarf and join us at the cabin."

"I want to wear the new scarf," said Lars, but in French, so Sita left it to Pierre to chide him. When she buckled him into the car seat of the rental, though, she wrapped it around him. The traffic was heavy and slow, ten-deep at the roundabout. Everyone wanted to be elsewhere.

*

They set up the grill and lay out the blankets on the lake shore as she drifted into the woods. Her road had been quiet, growing up. The neighbors across the road had a pool they never seemed to go in until late at night, as if they lived in some mosquito-free paradise—as if they lived here, she realized—and if a car drove into the cul-de-sac in error, it soon found its way out again. Bhoo-mija hadn't lived close enough to walk, and when she'd stayed over on a Friday night, or longer, if her parents needed to go out of town—if there was a wedding or a funeral, what else?—they'd sat on her bed, away from her gaggle of smaller siblings and the videogame console and the ping pong table, away from her parents' friends speaking a language Sita didn't understand and Bhoomija didn't bother to translate because what they had to say was always so boring, and Sita remembered how she'd lay awake at night, afraid to risk a trip to the bathroom for fear of hearing a child cry, or her own name interspersed among the conversation—"Sita, chhi!"—or her own footsteps.

She'd overshot the rose apple tree again: the sun was sneaking in amongst the trees, so the lake must be near. But after a series of retreats and advances Sita wasn't sure. The cabin was by a lake, in the woods, but that didn't mean the woods were endless on either side. She was going in circles, maybe. Morten had praised her, once, for finding the lake. That was what she would do now. Then she'd simply go back the way she'd planned to.

"Your friend is very sad, Chuha," her father had told her. "Every month she tells me how much she misses you, but when she came with her friend, that skateboarding boy, to have tea on Christmas I saw that she has gotten very thin."

Bhoomija regularly calling Sita's father, and calling on him, was more jarring than Bhoomija losing weight, but Sita hadn't pointed this out. After her mother, her father had gotten sick, and by the time he had recovered and gotten his shots, her aunts and uncles and cousins—and Bhoomija's, she supposed—had gotten sick, until Pierre had stopped asking her to disambiguate one mausi from another when he'd relayed the news. She hadn't gotten closer to the water, she realized; the whirring was the overdone, surely, grinding of moose teeth on green leaves. There were two, no, three in the clearing; one was smaller than the others, and Sita exhaled. She didn't know what one called a baby moose in any language, but if both generations were accounted for she knew she had nothing to fear.

"Deepa Auntie told me something in confidence and I want to tell you, now, in confidence," her father had said.

"Log kya kehenge?" she'd quipped, then stopped. If Bhoomija had decided to start taking drugs she was certainly not going to help Auntie stage an intervention. They'd drank bhang together with some desi muscle bros at the Diwali function senior year, and though Bhoomija had mocked Sita's wide-eyed delight, Sita could picture her popping pharmaceuticals while the printer ran all night, sending out summonses in a Jessie Spano frenzy. Once she sorted herself out would she regret the invitation?

"Chuha, Bhoomija is being investigated by the police. Do you remember that film with Kajol's nephew and that girl? That girl thinks that Bhoomija has shamed her by stealing her idea for a Ramayana update and creating something so lewd, and she has gotten the law involved somehow. You know that there is still very bad ventilation in these New York jails, beti, we can't let her end up there. Now they have finally given you shots; now you can come and stay with Bhoomija and make sure she eats properly until this case is finished. Make sure she is strong."

She had sat down on the unmade bed. "Why isn't Micah making sure she eats properly?"

"Auntie thinks he may be living with her, yes. But you know

Bhoomija, always full of secrets." Sita didn't want to laugh. She hadn't wanted her body on a satire either—Bhoomija swore it was earnest, though that seemed to be what a satirist would do when they weren't sure the joke was going to land—but this was America (this wasn't America, she noted, pulling the duvet cover over her thighs), so what other blaspheming had Bhoomija gotten up to? Sita realized she must have missed the first issue of the magazine, with whatever it said. It was unforgiveable.

It was unforgiveable yet Bhoomija had emailed her, afterwards, with no attached pdf copy, no link to follow to read; only, and repeatedly: you owe me a visit, child bride.

She had mumbled something to her father about how far it was to get to the city for the swabs she'd need to fly back, how expensive the travel was, and she had to pass language exams before she could work in an office again, and then she'd ask Pierre, she would, and, finally just: Lars, and as she watched the sleek brown family of three look at one another, unspeaking, and exit west, she let her cheeks burn at his reply. "You can leave Lars with me and go and see her. I am better now."

The moose seemed not to mind being followed, and when she came upon the tree she watched them sniff it, and think it wanting, and move forward into the shadowed foliage. She plucked the fruit, one in each palm, and sat on the ground as though she had just seen a sick man, and an old man, and a dead man. If she took a bite and held it in her mouth, she could appreciate the quiet, the swell of pride that in the village comingled with her own knotted self-regard. She'd done it; Bhoomija had really done it.

When she took the other rose apple into her mouth and swallowed it whole she felt herself disappear, and—for more than a moment—she was happy.

*

When she awoke she was in the leafy shade, a bitten rose apple in her left hand, and Pierre was shaking her shoulders. Behind him she could hear the children, and Morten's crashing footsteps, and the crushed twigs under the stroller's massive tires. When he saw her eyes had opened, he must not have liked what he saw, she thought, for it took him another second to stop shaking. "We're heading back for the fireworks," he said, as though it was a reminder.

They'd never been together for the Fourth, but Sita knew Pierre would be wonderful at a fireworks show: he'd swing his arms around them and remember to tie a towel around Lars' ears and buy him ice cream on a stick. He'd see the shapes themselves as graceful reminders of the ephemerality of beauty, and the added importance impermanence bestowed. It was something she'd loved about him: he'd never once pretended to like yoga to meet pretty white girls, but when he'd watched her stretch in the mornings, he'd caught on right away. Hang was as secular as they came, and he said he was, too, but Sita knew his obsession with the way things looked came from a misplaced concern for the way things were and could be. She willed her mouth to smile, her feet to point into the earth and accept her weight, but then there was her hand, the missing rose apple, the taken bite.

How long had it been since she had been well? How much of her life needed to be unpurled before she could be rendered anew?

Lars, hurtling through the clearing, stopped at his father's shoulder, extended his little hand. They were three, together, and safe.

When Bhoomija talked about what Sita owed, she wasn't talking about their friendship. For Bhoomija it had always been about community, and, woven together, country. Pierre, parachuted in, flown out: she was free of his past, and he of hers. All he wanted for her was what men had always asked of Sitas: to be good, to be beloved, to be fertile. It was too bad Lars wasn't twins, but Sita hadn't split up Lav and Kush, and without both would the Kosalan empire have stood as strong? The Kosalan empire wasn't what she needed to be thinking about right now, Bhoomija would have said. Videha may be across the sea but it still existed. She still existed. And if they had wrought destruction, well, maybe that had been their purpose all along. But—thought Sita:

Lars. Who I have made beautiful, and strong, and fit for purpose: a prince amongst these wraiths. Who I have made, Bhoomija.

She tucked the half-eaten rose apple in his palm, and swerved so her mouth was aimed elsewhere, and vomited.

"Mumma?"

"Dekho, munna, vriksh," she whispered, wiping her mouth.

"Go and take Ronja and see if you can find Signe anywhere, Captain Sabertooth," Morten said, as Pierre shook her once more. "I think they're being held captive by the nefarious Luna, and you must save them. Your pappa can push the stroller, and you can help him find his way."

When he spoke next, his voice was pitched lower, and Sita felt most of it get sucked into the soil, and the porous bark, and her fingertips. "Stella, don't flail." He took hold of her not by her honed shoulders but with an arm under her back, an arm under her knees. If she opened her mouth his beard would trail into it. She was lying still, and she was moving, and when he cocked his elbow under her ear to turn her head away from his face she saw the forest as though she was a low-flying bird.

"I want to stay here," she thought, and, catching sight of the rippled mirror-face of the lake approaching, shafts of sunlight easing themselves between the trunks of the silver birches, said so before it was too late.

"No one is stopping you," said Morten. At the edge of the water

Sita braced herself for ground impact and, when she felt his fingers tighten around her, turned her head into his elbow, her eyes to his. He held her in his glance as he lowered himself onto the sand, Sita with him, and when he pulled his legs out from under her and his phone out of his pocket, moved his fingers and his gaze towards his texts, she felt her cheeks still burning and closed her eyes. She felt, rather than heard, the first firework, and then the second.

He patted her on the head like Pierre had once done Nenn. "Sleep, Stella," he said, and she did, and when the final rockets burst against her temple he patted her head until she woke and lead her back to his cabin, the rose apple, her son.

12

The other side of the fjord formed a fence around Sita's life. Green today, as the summer drifted, snow-tipped year-round, anything but gentle. The ripe Onam moon, nesting in a corner of the sky, peeked out from behind the mountains that almost always faced her. It was warm and she was alone. She was always alone, nearly always; perhaps it was just that the stocky boats kept to schedule, but she hadn't joined Mona and Signe and Ronja, tiny as a Saturday sweet, on their trips this summer to watch the surfing. Lars was lording it over his daycare. Pierre was turning straw into gold in his glass-walled office.

When he came out she was waiting for him on a bench by the water. He spotted her instantly though from the back, now, she looked like a stranger, molten curves piled atop one another in pilled yarn. When he kissed her atop her head and then under her ear she felt the heat he'd transferred off her hair.

"I made this," she said, though it was an exaggeration; she held it up on its needles, so perhaps it was so evidently false it didn't count as a lie.

"Mmm," said Pierre.

"For us to sit on, on a picnic tomorrow. The summer's almost gone and we've hardly sat in the sun together." It was brown and orange and red so anything Lars smeared on it would disappear into the chevrons.

"Oh! Thanks!" He took her hand, but pulled her up instead of sitting beside her; he began to walk rather quickly in the direction of the daycare and Sita realized he must have worked until the last minute. The sun told them nothing these days until it was quite late; Lars would sleep and Pierre would slip away for a dip as it feigned setting.

When Lars had been wrested from his admirers Pierre walked them onwards, away from the sea and the empty kitchen and the stew Sita'd seen packed away in the fridge to be reheated, the dry rolls. "Où allons-nous?" asked Lars. "Aurai-je besoin de mon chapeau?" While he went to fetch the hat Pierre and Sita stood facing the care center, and she saw him looking at her sideways, carefully, and wished he would take her hand. But Lars returned and claimed Pierre's fingers, his gait quick but slightly wobbly. Still, there was another hand. To reach it she would have to put Pierre in the center, distance herself from Lars.

When they reached the top of the hill, Pierre told Lars to run up and down seven times as fast as he could, and took the needles from her hand and spread the t-shirt yarn across the grass and sat. She joined him even though it meant an unraveling beneath her. The hill was dotted with tiny yellow draba, which wouldn't leave a mark on his chin yet Sita wished she could try nonetheless. "Why wait for a picnic?" Pierre asked her.

Without food, without yarn, there was nothing to do with her fingers, and she tucked them beneath her thighs and joined Pierre in watching the sky, the town flung out beneath them, thoughtlessly, if compact. If it had been beautiful things would have gone differently between them, she thought. She ran her fingers over the interlocked cotton, poking holes in it, for it would be unspooled by twilight.

"How's Mona?" Pierre asked.

"Wonderful," Sita said.

"Morten can't wait til it's his turn out of the office," Pierre said.

"I'll bet," she said. Lars was slowing down now—perhaps he'd done seven; could he count?—but she angled her body to Pierre. "I can make dinner tomorrow. Kitchdi. I'll soak the daal tonight."

"That sounds great," he said, and pulled Lars onto the blanket.

In the evening she poured the pulses through her fingers, checking for mold, but there was nothing. She let them soak.

*

The day had passed. Lars had pitched a fit when Pierre explained that the three of them would be going for a picnic instead of heading out to the cabin, sans Sita, with Uncle Morten. While she was adding the chonk, the doorbell rang, and Lars leapt upon Morten like a tiny Hanuman. Mona was pushing the baby, supine, and Signe, holding onto some kind of stroller-affixed scooter Sita imagined Pierre coveting. Signe's lips were cherry-red around a lollipop, and Mona held one out for Lars.

"We thought we'd drop by like Americans," Mona said.

"For an Utepils," Morten added.

Pierre proclaimed white wine a better fit for the khichdi, and they ate out of tiny bowls to mask the insufficiency of the fare. Mona helped Sita take the sheets off the line on the porch while the boys wrangled the children. "It's Rakhi," Sita told Mona, explaining the bracelets. "Do you think my brothers will send me money?"

"I thought you were an only child," Mona said, spreading them out on the sofa as though preparing to paint. Sita draped the pillowcases over the counter, careful to avoid the crackers Pierre had taken out in place of papadum, the chopped lemons he'd taken out in place of aachaar.

"Cousin brothers," Sita amended. She'd sent over friendship bracelets as a child, gotten airmail envelopes unfolded to reveal drawings of trains and then towers and then robots. After she'd forgotten to send over bracelets she'd blush when the envelopes continued to arrive, this time with sheets of bindis or ludicrous laminated cards with cartoon bears on, and sentimental poems. When she was younger she'd wanted them to visit, just once, even if it would mean losing a month in India, where maids would bring her water (and then her mother would yell at her for asking them to).

"Signe and Ronja have plenty of cousin brothers," Mona said, "but it's not enough for Morten. He wishes Ronja were a boy."

Her parents had never wished she were a boy, she was sure of it. She didn't think, either, that they regretted her accent, her unbraided hair, her short-lived obsession with plastic chokers when she had an entire caboodle full of ornate gold and silver jewelry. She was their Chuha. Her father wanted her to do what she wanted, even when it was boring; her mother wanted her to speak in quips, like Lorelai Gilmore, and idolize her, and go out to diners with her and to town hall meetings and open-air theatres. She'd been lucky; her mother was too busy to push. If they were both free on a Saturday, and they were caught up on ZeeTV and were between holidays, they would go to the mall and share a pretzel and talk about how next time this happened, they should go rollerblading. Pierre had taken her rollerblading the week before Valentine's Day. He'd read about a dinky hall in the burbs that did midnight hip hop hours and they'd checked their parkas in the cloakroom and swapped their boots for the rink's loaners, and though they could both skate without needing assistance they held hands and, less feasibly, he'd place his palm on the small of her back and try to spin her. She'd told her mom about it—she wasn't in the habit of sharing the content of her liaisons with her mother, but the form, that seemed safe—and her mother laughed, and sipped her tea, and told her she was jealous.

"Not jealous," Sita suggested. It wasn't nostalgic, either, what her mother meant. They hadn't been able to put their finger on it before they'd ended the call.

Her father had been more considered in his praise of Pierre. "You'll have so many options," he'd told her.

"How many photos did you see before you chose mom?" she'd asked, knowing it was a cheap rebuttal, apples to oranges. But Pierre had taken her hair, strand by strand, and lain it on the silk pillowcase he'd bought for her at Macy's, and whispered, "You look just like Aaliyah." If she could have a line-up of such men, then she'd want a swayamvara. As it was she hadn't been sure she'd have the option of Pierre for more than a few months. It would be a year in June since he'd graduated, and if he wanted they would transfer him to a European office; he'd mentioned, once, having her fly out to visit him in Prague.

By March things had changed, and after they'd met Pierre

they'd called her again. "Let's at least see if someone has a red lengha you can borrow," her mother said. "They can leave it on their front porch. You can do a zoom." But though she'd made a go at her own mehndi she'd worn the lengha she'd worn to everything else. She'd e-mailed her mother the pictures, and her mother had e-mailed her cousins, and later, after she'd gone, Micah had e-mailed her a picture of a battered package with a blue velvet box inside containing a silver coin, Ganesh-emblazoned, and by now, she supposed, he had spent it.

*

The next day Mona rang her doorbell while the boys were at church. When Sita ignored it she rapped on the kitchen window and then stuck her hand through—it was open, and as Mona drew back the curtain Sita could feel the breeze come in off the water. The climb up the mountain would be pleasant, at first, and then blistering, and Sita grabbed her cardigan and the new scarf as she opened the door.

Mona wasn't even wearing sneakers. "I brought string this time," she said, stepping inside. "I thought we could make Rakhi bracelets."

For a moment Sita tried to picture what rocky bracelets could be, conjuring gems, and then she hung her gear back up and closed the door. Mona had swung her rucksack up onto her hip and was pulling primary colors—blue, orange, purple—out of it. "Is Ronja at church today, then?"

Mona shook her head. "With my parents, actually, both the girls. They're having a waffle date. But in the afternoon I thought Signe could tie one on Lars."

For a moment Sita felt as though time had stopped, but this wasn't where time stopped: inside the dour house, on the still side of the closed door. She sat down and tried to hear her breath.

"Okay, look, it was just an idea. No problem. We could just have coffee—"

"Mona. Stop. I would love to make rakhis with you. I'd love for Signe to tie one on Lars. Though you know that means they'll never be sweethearts." She tried to wipe her eyes with her shirt, but it was gross, tough, and she dug into the basket of hats and gloves and sunglasses where she knew Pierre had left a half-empty water bottle, and she dabbed her shirt into it and wiped the tears off her face. Mona crouched down and swallowed her up, it felt like. "Mona, it's fine. I'm fine."

Mona disengaged but plopped herself down and tilted her head. "It's been awhile, you know."

"I know," Sita said.

"Did you and Bhoomija exchange rakhis?"

"That's not really how it works."

"Well, what did you do?"

But they hadn't done anything. They'd planned, they'd plotted. They'd teamed up to be partners in the dances for functions, held the other's horrible crushes in whatever esteem necessary, stared at the stars together and wondered when they'd stare at the stars with boys, and then, when they were asked, promised one another they'd never run off to stare at the stars with boys if they'd already made plans. "We ate the parts of the prasad the other one hated," Sita said. Until Bhoomija had stopped taking any, had disentangled her thoughts about the cosmos from her thoughts about the small white building with its ornately carved roof, brilliant in the flat sun of their childhood, teeming with people who had taken a good look at the catalog of gods and goddesses and sexual manuals and deeply existential questions and chosen caste as what they'd cling to most dearly in the middle of the cornfields.

"I don't know what pra ... anyways. I'm sorry. Yesterday it sounded like, well, I just figured you might not want to be alone."

Sita wanted to laugh. Rakhi, of all days? It was always sunny on Rakhi, nearly always warm, and all it meant, really, was the promise of envelopes in the mail. She knew she'd mentioned other holidays to Mona. They'd known one another for multiple Diwalis, for gods' sake. But this is what it came down to: not laughing. Not crying. "Let's get knotting."

*

She didn't tell Mona, the following weekend, about Janmashtmi. For Sita this would forever be Lars' real birthday. This whole week he'd been wearing the bracelets Mona had made, gifts of equal measure to those Signe wore—a more feminist Rakhi than that of her childhood. These are his friends, she knew. This is his family. She had no stomach for dressing him up in a crown, guiding him to play with his little wooden whistle, the closest she'd found to a flute. Sixteen years to go, she counted, as though she'd done anything more than move out at eighteen. Well, she'd stayed out.

She was the youngest in her office by far; that fateful March, Micah had decamped to his parents', and she'd nestled into Pierre to the sounds of ambulance sirens as her colleagues set up their home offices in the burbs. In Bhoomija's crowd it was the opposite; she called to rant and rave about it, but once, after Sita heard the tail end of a fractious conversation through the bedroom walls, she'd texted Sita a screenshot of incoming flights, LGA - MDW. There's nothing special about New York if all the agents are working from home, she wrote. Come over, Sita had responded. You can hide under my bed until you're ready to join us in it. We can surprise Pierre with a threesome.

I'm not the one who needs to sleep with every idiot who compliments my hair, wrote Bhoomija.

Too bad, Sita'd written, your hair's great. But it had hurt. She hadn't responded to Bhoomija's brown thumbs up; she'd waited until she had wedding pictures to send to text next. There hadn't been congratulations. Just: I'm putting together an artists' commune in my place here in case things go south. There's a girl named Urvashi who might bring a car. There's a dude named Suraj who once had a cartoon in the *New Yorker*.

Today they went north, just the three of them, Pierre letting Lars take the lead. It was early in the day, and the woods were quiet. There was a clearing Pierre knew about where they'd be more likely to see a stag, if Lars could be convinced of the necessity to stay quiet. He recapped his week, his month, his year, his life, as they walked on. Pierre took pictures for Hang: he texted her extracts of the immediate past, the best parts. When she'd texted the wedding photos to her parents, her mother had texted back with emoji: another mother tongue Sita barely spoke. Her father waited until the next day and called from the mailbox to tell her that her mother was sick. He'd been looking forward to peaceful days working from home, he'd said; now she was coughing and moaning, and he was about to make rajma chawal himself for the first time since she'd been little and her mother run ragged. As per request, he added, so Sita didn't tell him to quit being a martyr and order a pizza.

Tomorrow I'll bring food, she said. Pierre had made them a wedding feast, just falafel but she'd thought that last time, her mom had appreciated his dab hand with the spices. She'd been planning on stopping by on the way to the airport, since they'd be renting a car to get there. She was legally wed now, but she figured they'd be settled in by summer, sorted enough up north to fly back to her parents' and do the pheras and the garlands at the gazebo on their back lawn. Micah would probably cater if his school would let him use their kitchens. Pasta, maybe. Pierre's mother would come, and she might not like Indian. Pierre had argued that it didn't matter, which meant she didn't, and of course it did. As long as she didn't catch her mother's cough she wouldn't have any trouble at the airport.

She drove; Pierre was anxious, now, one foot off the continent. They made record time, and when they got to the neighborhood, Pierre asked if she minded if he waited on the porch, but her father was already on the porch, two rajais on top of his coat. She asked Pierre to wait with the car; they shouldn't leave their passports unattended.

"It's bad," her father said as she approached, before she'd asked. Then: "Sita, don't go."

"What?" She'd gone inside to avoid looking at him, found her mother sleeping in a batik nightie she'd complimented Bhoomija's mother on, and received as a gift the next birthday. She didn't look small, or beleaguered. There was water beside the table, the latest Dalrymple. Two sets of glasses.

Her mother twitched in her sleep. Sorry, she mouthed.

Their steps were muffled now; she hadn't seen cairns for ages, and hoped Pierre understood where they were. Lars had grown tired of stomping his way through the undergrowth and started climbing; on their next Paris trip, Pierre suggested, he would take Lars to the zoo. In winter? It would still be warmer than here, still lighter, and more jolly. And weren't they jolly? Pierre asked, and Sita had to admit that they were.

13

They spoke in Norwegian now with one another; Mona slowly, overenunciating, Sita as fast she could manage. The exam was on Thursday and Friday, for having come up this far the examiners were in no hurry, it seemed, to leave their expense-account hotel rooms, and had scheduled her to write first, speak after. Mona would speed up when she talked to Ronja, and then slow down for her, and though Sita might have explained that she understood what Mona told her daughter, she didn't know what use it would be. Mona was happy, sometimes. She'd been tapped to sponsor a new energy drink featuring a sea creature, or a sea plant, on this point Sita couldn't be sure, and they had all come to the harbor to wait for the ferry to take them across to where the poster image would be shot: Mona and Morten and the girls, and Pierre and Lars and Sita, and a gaggle of ad makers who weren't so much younger than them but had the ironed, still pimply appearance of people from the south, their hair dyed a purplish black color that left Morten the odd one out for once. Lars was handing out flowers, singing the southerners a song about murderous bears, charming them all with his dialect. Signe was in her pushchair, asleep, and though Morten carried Ronja in a holster on his chest, Mona kept glancing at her.

This wasn't the ferry that they'd come on: Pierre and Sita, the southerners, Mona's parents. It was a smaller ship and went back and forth to the islands, and Sita had taken it countless weekends to watch Mona dance atop the waves but this deep into the fall, the windows were shut and the southerners sat at a distance from them, breathing as shallowly as they could. "He's still upset," Mona was whispering to her, and then she repeated it in English and Sita turned her eyes away from the waves at to her. "I thought things would wear off by now—she can hold her head up, she can smile. She's so smiley, Sita! And so alert! Look at her studying Pierre's new haircut."

"I wish he'd come around," Sita agreed, but as it was Morten, weakly. He was talking to Pierre and Lars, presumably no longer about flowers or bears, and holding a bottle of the advertised energy drink and taking in long draughts like some kind of overfed knight.

"Pierre would have loved a girl," Mona said, following her gaze, and her voice was so sad Sita looked back at her.

"You're allowed to be angry about this," Sita said.

Mona laughed. "My mother says I should give it a few years."

Sita looked at Morten, the way he had Lars sitting at attention. "You shouldn't."

Another chuckle. "He'll come around."

Morten looked at them and winked and gave Lars a sip of the bright green drink. Sita supposed Mona winked back; how was she to know?

It was Durga Puja, and if nothing else—certainly, on this desolate island, there would be nothing else—Sita decided to hike where she could, salute the desperately clinging sun, and sing a bhajan where no one could hear. If Durga wasn't her mother, it didn't matter; she'd never felt a sense of communion with the aunties and uncles standing next to her in the aarti crowd, never thought they were praying to the same maternal force even though, after all, they used the same names: Durga, Ganga, Gadhimai, Ma. They spoke the same languages, but past each other. There were many paths to god, the panditji liked to say, and she thought hers must be hers alone.

Before she met Pierre, Bhoomija liked to bring up Sita's Gadhimai summers at parties. "You think y'all are tough?" she'd ask. "Sita has you all beat. This shakti-powered Goddess could slit your throat." She'd pepper her story with words Sita knew Bhoomija took solace in, had reclaimed for her own: not only shakti, but mindfulness, self-actualization. She'd tell Sita to prove it by doing a backbend, as if her yoga ability corroborated the narrative.

Sita'd done it: eyes on her.

The last Durga Puja before she'd left had fallen early; she'd taken the train in from the city, even though her parents were on call, unable to trek to the mandir. Her mother had gotten called in, and as she cleaned up the kitchen with her father he'd hummed the aarti, and she'd joined in. She knew she was a rarity, an only child and an only girl, at that, but if her father thought this was a pity he'd never made her feel it. They'd sat in front of the turned-off television and her father had suggested they go to Europe for her mother's fiftieth: not just stop over, as they used to on his way home, but gratuitously. That was what made things special: gratuitousness, superfluity. When the Gadhimai sacrifice came to an end—and Sita knew they would come to an end—something would be lost, and perhaps it would be something she'd found crucial, but nothing the world needed. Nothing this place needed so much as Morten, and Mona, and their beautiful flag-covered children.

When she saw him come over the ridge her heart didn't beat faster, her shoulders were still, her breath at ease. "They're starting soon," Morten said. "She wants you there." He kept his distance, and Sita wished he would ask her what she had been singing, knew he wouldn't, wanted to tell him. Didn't. "She's in a mood today." He did step forward, then, and Sita found her heart in her throat, and when he bent down at her feet, he said, "See, look where you're stepping? That root—it'll be cloudberry in the spring. If we come and pick it before anybody else we can make jam."

She looked down at him.

"Have you ever had cloudberry jam, Stella?"

She crouched beside him. The ground looked empty—okay, no, a slip of greenish brown. She'd never had cloudberry jam. If she went home now she'd never have it. "What if we dug up the root and planted it in the village?" she asked.

He stared at her. Horrified? His face was impassive, normal. "One could do that," he said. "Let's not today."

He took her hands to drag her up and Sita felt herself lean forward, saw herself kiss him, felt the rough of his lips and his beard smother her face.

Then she was on the ground, not pushed but released with a force that felled her. He was up and didn't stoop to help her. "Let's get back to the others."

When she stayed to finish her singing, he didn't come back for her. When she returned to the shoot, it was over, and they were gathered at the pier, and neither Mona nor Morten looked at her as she approached. Until Pierre handed her a beer, she wasn't sure that he'd kept mum.

*

For Halloween they came to the house, all four of them, Signe dressed up in a new crocheted princess dress that Sita didn't remember being asked about, and certainly hadn't made. Ronja was asleep under a knit blanket, black with little orange pom-poms. She could have taught Mona how to make them pumpkins. She hadn't known they were coming, but Pierre, taking dozens of tiny little ramekins from the fridge, seemed to have prepared. She sat on the ground with Mona and the tots; Mona played the Monster Mash from her phone, over and over again, and made little faces which Lars copied, squealing. Morten and Pierre were on the couch, discussing what, she did not know.

Tomorrow was Karva Chauth, which wouldn't be improved by a hangover, but nor could it be made worse, surely, so she drank a half glass of wine between each sorry olive, grown perhaps in a glass box nowhere near the Mediterranean. Pierre had kept the curtains open, and the moon, almost full in the sky, hung low and blue over the water. Mona was talking about work, not her own but their husbands', and Sita wasn't sure why she didn't just go to the couch where they would understand. The written exam had gone fine, but the oral examiner's questions had been such that she didn't know what to say: What do you like to do with your time? How has living in Norway changed you? In the end she had remembered about Mona, and talked about her new secondhand love of surfing, and passed. Now you can take your citizenship test, said the examiner, though you'll have to study. If you're not from a country with a robust higher education system then it can be a challenge, he said. Sita told him about her degree, and he said, "Well, then, you needn't bother. You'll likely be gone soon. After all, there's nothing for an anthropologist to study here."

It became clear, upon inspection, that Mona was in costume. "Indiana Jones!" Sita said.

Mona stopped mid-sentence. Well, Sita supposed, she'd interrupted. But Mona was smiling, if weakly. "Yes, see, you understood it immediately. At least I can stop popping into the office whenever I feel like it; poor Pierre has no choice."

She hadn't realized that Pierre had worn a costume, but of course he must have; he must still be wearing one. She looked at him and at Lars: matching A-Rods. Had she been given a hat, too? There was one hanging by the door, sharing the hook with her scarf. "I should get that," she whispered, and when she rose, she could feel the wine—she'd bypassed sweet relief and gone straight to a doom that hit below the stomach.

Mona rose with her, took her arm. Now that their mouths and ears were farther from the children she spoke a bit more loudly. "Morten said he laughed it off. Well, Morten said that Morten laughed it off. You should talk to Pierre."

"He's upset that they didn't know A-Rod? Why would they?"

Mona shook her head, spoke more slowly. "No, like I said: when I explained who I was they said he was my little Asian side-kick, and you must be his little temple whore."

"Oh," said Sita.

"When we were taking off our shoes I asked him if he was going to go to HR, but he shrugged. Sometimes I hate this place."

Sita put the hat on. "Well, Pierre loves it."

"Sita," said Mona.

When they gave the children candy, Lars was flabbergasted. "It's Tuesday!" he repeated, pouring the smarties into his mouth like Sita quite wanted to do. Pierre caught her eye and blew her a kiss. She blew one back: his little temple whore.

*

The moon was up all day in November, so for a second Sita considered not fasting at all. Lars had insisted on wearing matching hats with his papa again, so Pierre'd gone back to work in his Short Round costume; as she'd waved them off Sita'd winced. Pierre was a wonderful father, she considered. She'd better at least skip breakfast. The Ahoi fast was at the end of the week, when the moon was halved, like her heart.

Mona had cornered her at drop-off; she'd pleaded a headache— a headache she truly had—and escaped. They could both knit now, though the bright colors and bold patterns that Mona chose made her sloppy errors unavoidable. When Mona had suggested that a coffee might help, tilted her head towards the café next to the shop that now specialized, it seemed, in cheap and brittle dishware too fragile to carry home in the slightest wind, she'd shaken her head, and said, "fasting," though coffee, after all, was permitted.

The hail was sharp against her eyes, and she bought a brimmed shapka she'd seen arrive in the shop closest the harbor last week and wore it in an attempt to scale the hill, but though the hail looked like grit it was not. There were no sticks to be found, and anyway, at the top she'd be further assailed. In the third shop the cashier had asked about Lars, and she found that their children were classmates, that Marit Helene came home every day and gushed about Lars over her brown cheese dosa. After that, she couldn't step into the fourth. There was nowhere else.

In the fishmongers', Morten's parents' hair was fading, red to grey. The shrimp men at the harbor shook their heads at her, who never bought anything, not once. Where the hot dog stand would be, come summer, the village tidiers had pushed the snow into a large pile worthy of scaling up and sliding down. There was little fog today, and the lighthouse sputtered and blinked.

If she made it back home she would take in another mongoose

and name it after her mother. That way when Bhoomija got home from her zine-making days she could step inside and see: Micah, making them dinner. Tara, their mongoose, asleep in front of the fire. Sita wouldn't mention that she'd had a mongoose before, had a mother before. No one would mention Lars. If Bhoomija ever had a baby, it would be a daughter named Shakti, and no one would ever mispronounce her name.

The scene carried her onto the ferry, not the one to the islands, but the one to the city down the coast, where they could catch a train to the airport. She bought a coffee and, sitting down by a seat next to a window out of which nothing was visible but hail and darkness, unwrapped her scarf. Micah and Bhoomija and Tara and Shakti. A full house all on its own, without any flotsam. Still. She'd been summoned, hadn't she?

The waves made the ship tilt, and she picked up the coffee too late, and it sloshed on the brimmed table and over it, onto the frayed edges of her paisley scarf specially resuscitated and the rounded center of her body as it pushed itself between the seat and the table. She thumbed the coffee off the darkened wool and hoped, if she was being looked at now, that she didn't look sallow. That she looked like a woman who knew where she was going. That she looked like Sita come out of her furrow. No, like Sita come out of her fire.

The boat threaded itself through the fjord, not at all becalmed, and she decided to buy something to eat.

*   *   *

ACKNOWLEDGMENTS

This book owes a debt of gratitude towards every Ramayana discussed in Paula Richman's *Many Ramayanas*, as well as towards that book itself; it also could not have existed without Amar Chitra Katha's version of *The Panchatantra* and the writings of Rasma Haidri, Khalid Hussain, Mahmona Khan, Zashan Shakar, and the *I Dine Sko/Tumhari Nazar Se/In Your Shoes* anthology.

Thank you to Jowan Mohammed, James Nikopoulos, and the BL Thursday writers group, whose thoughts on this story helped it take shape. Thank you, also, to *A-Minor Magazine*, *Flash Flood*, *Midnight Breakfast*, and *The VIDA Review* for giving a home to sections of Sita's story, and to *No Contact Mag* and *Present Tense* for finding space for other words from the universe in which the story is set. Thank you, finally, to Misha Rai, Cassie Mannes Murray, and everyone at Miami University Press who helped make this story a book, to Nord University, for bringing me north, and to the friends and family who understood why I stayed as long as I could.

ABOUT THE AUTHOR

Rashi Rohatgi is the author of the prize-winning novella *Where the Sun Will Rise Tomorrow* and the first English translator of the seminal Mauritian novel *Blood-Red Sweat*. Her writing has been supported by *Bread Loaf*, *Tin House*, *VONA*, *Sewanee*, and AWP. Originally from Pennsylvania, she now lives in Norway.